The Seed *of* SIMEON

Simon of Cyrene

Dr. John E. Bell

ISBN 979-8-89345-612-7 (paperback)
ISBN 979-8-89345-613-4 (digital)

Copyright © 2024 by Dr. John E. Bell

All rights reserved. No part of this publication may be reproduced, distributed, or transmitted in any form or by any means, including photocopying, recording, or other electronic or mechanical methods without the prior written permission of the publisher. For permission requests, solicit the publisher via the address below.

Christian Faith Publishing
832 Park Avenue
Meadville, PA 16335
www.christianfaithpublishing.com

Printed in the United States of America

DEDICATION

I dedicate this book to my daughter Amber and all my family, including my mother, siblings, nieces, nephews, and cousins. I love you all.

This is also dedicated to all my friends, Phi-Beta-Sigma Fraternity Brothers and Zeta Sorority Sisters, the Christian Church Community, and colleagues who believe this book could be a reality from my vision of the power of God.

I want to also dedicate this book to all the future generations of my children and their children that I may never live to see. I love you all now and forever; love is the true gift I give you in my mortal life and beyond my life toward my eternal walk with God.

ACKNOWLEDGMENT

I want to acknowledge the people who believed in my book project and supported me as I took over ten years to write this story. This labor of love involved research, countless days of historical references, and a focus on the sensitivity of race, culture, and history of such an interesting concept. Though this is a fictional narrative, it embellishes this story from a very real savior, Jesus Christ, and his passion to redeem mankind from its sins.

CONTENTS

Acknowledgment v

Chapter 1: Introduction of the Sacred Act that Transformed the Life of Simon of Cyrene, Simeon of Niger 1

Chapter 2: The Challenge of Power 13

Chapter 3: The Militant and Powerful Protectors of the Sworn Sacred Oath of Simon 16

Chapter 4: The Blood Of The Innocent..................................22

Chapter 5: The Miraculous Events of Modern Times even with Abandoned Disbelief..............................28

Chapter 6: Rise of the Sacred League of Death and Destruction ...38

Chapter 7: Revelation of a Divine Prophesy over the Science of Evil 44

Chapter 8: Echoes of a Dark Pursuit 52

Chapter 9: Veiled Dangers 74

Chapter 10: The Legacy of The Living Saint..............................85

CHAPTER 1

Introduction of the Sacred Act that Transformed the Life of Simon of Cyrene, Simeon of Niger

In the year of our Lord AD 32, the observation of Passover in Jerusalem was being held. Amid the bustling city, a choir's harmonious voices echoed in the background, adding a touch of serenity to the vivid tableau. Jerusalem was celebrating Passover at the time, and Simon, of Jewish heritage, entered Jerusalem to participate. He was not alone; he was accompanied by his wife, Bayla, and his two kids, Rufus and Alexander. The youngest, Rufus, was fourteen years old, while Alexander was sixteen. Both of them were prized in Simon and their mother's eyes.

Simon, on the other hand, was no ordinary figure. Being 5'10" and with brown eyes that gleamed with wisdom, he had a remarkable appearance. His skin was a tribute to his ancestry, with an equal tone ranging from a lovely chocolate brown to a rich black shade. His hair was as dark as the stars at midnight, kinky and curly, and clearly of African descent.

His presence reverberated with the weight of history, and his body was marked by the experiences and knowledge he had gathered over the years. His fluctuating weight between 185 and 220 pounds was evidence of a life full of physical and spiritual experiences.

Between the ages of thirty-two and thirty-six, Simon, as he was called, was a man in the prime of his life. His name, derived from the Hebrew interpretation, meant "people of color" or, more simply, "Black." His presence in this historic city served as a reminder of humanity's diversity and interconnectedness, echoing the rich tapestry of history that had woven people from all walks of life together.

As they were standing on the outskirts of Jerusalem, Bayla embraced her husband, Simon, kissed him, and then looked out at the city in front of them. Bayla's deep brown eyes, which were giddy with excitement, made the happiness quite evident. Compared to other people walking about Jerusalem, her olive-brown complexion was lovely. She was relatively young compared to Simon but always there for him.

On the other hand, Rufus and Alexander shared their parents' excitement at having arrived at their last destination. To show how happy he was, Rufus came up to his father and hugged him. All the family members smiled and embraced Simon as they looked at Jerusalem. Obviously, the entire family loved and respected Simon because he was the head of the family.

Simon, while looking at the beauty of the city of Jerusalem, said, "God has truly blessed me, and I am grateful to be able to celebrate this great time with you, Bayla, and my sons Rufus and Alexander. I thank God we came to Jerusalem from Cyrene to celebrate this great time for our people. I feel the Lord will forever bless us for our journey here, Bayla."

Bayla replied, "Yes, my Lord, it is a lovely time, and I, too, feel that the Lord has given us his mercy in our travels to the city of Jerusalem to observe Passover. We are all here, and I am excited to finally see the city of Jerusalem with my love and our family."

Even though Rufus was very happy to be in a new place, he was also very curious to find out why they traveled so much, and when Bayla mentioned Passover, he couldn't help asking, "Father, what is the Passover celebration all about in Jerusalem?"

Simon looked at Rufus, patted his head with love, and explained, "Rufus, today is the day that our people celebrate Passover, and it is a time that the Lord spared our people under the leadership of his servant Moses from the angel of death. This was a time when we were in bondage under Pharaoh Ramses in Egypt, a long time ago, my son."

Alexander, who was listening to all his family talk about Passover, asked excitedly, "Father, there are so many people moving throughout the city, and it seems there is some type of event going on down there. I wonder what could be going on?"

Little did they know that the hustle in the city was not because of a happy event or a celebration but because of the saddest event that was soon to be remembered by all. So, Simon replied unsurely, "I am not sure, Alexander. It may be part of the festivities around the Passover event or some procession of the people, but I truly cannot say Alexander."

Bayla also added, "Alexander, this is a unique time for the people of Israel and all the people that God spared all over this great area of Jerusalem. I am sure we will find out what is going on in the city of Jerusalem during this time of celebration and remembrance of the children of Israel. For the Lord has always provided for us."

Rufus was the curious one and always had questions to ask. And so, he questioned his father once again. "Father, were you one of the people that were a part of the children of Israel that were freed with Moses?"

The entire family, including Simon, laughed at Rufus's innocent question for his father while Rufus continued to look at Simon, waiting curiously for his father to answer. And Simon replied laughingly, "No, my son, I was not born at that time, and neither was your mother. But my family's parents were a part of the Exodus out of Egypt, and many of our kin lived many moons ago through that period; many crossed the Sea of Reeds and even lived in the land of Canaan. It is for this reason we celebrate this great time, my son."

As he was done talking, he hugged Rufus lovingly, appreciating his innocence.

Bayla affirmed to Rufus, saying, "Yes, Rufus, my son, that would make your mother very old and your father as old as the Pyramids in Egypt. We don't look that old, do we, son?"

They all once again laughed together and embraced the moment. Even though Alexander was actively listening and contributing to the conversation they were having as a family, his attention was constantly shifting to the chaos that was going on in the city as they all laughed and embraced the moment.

So, Alexander once again questioned his father impatiently, "Father, there seems to be a huge crowd gathering and moving out toward the city of Golgotha. I don't know if that is a part of Passover, but many people are assembling along the road."

Simon sighed. "I don't know my son. I know many events are taking place throughout Jerusalem today. I know I will be going into the city of Jerusalem today. I can only hope that I will not be away very long with all that will be going on today."

Bayla also explained, "Yes, your Father has to return and share in the first day of the feast of Passover with us all tonight." Then she looked at Simon and said, "I am sure the Lord will guide you, my love, and we will be looking for your safe return from Jerusalem today."

Rufus asked, "Father, will I ever be able to come with you to Jerusalem?"

Rufus was hopeful that his father would allow him to come with him today, but contrastingly, Simon replied, "Yes, and my son, you will be able to come one day. But today is the first day of Passover, and the markets will be filled with people from everywhere."

Rufus sighed. "Yes, Father, I will certainly help Mother today and await your return."

Bayla looked at Rufus with concern about his disappointment and understood that he was not content with his father's words. She then hugged Rufus, and after a while, she moved towards Simon, hugged him too, and said, "My love, our sons are growing up daily. Alexander is our oldest son, and Rufus is not very far behind."

"I feel you should allow Rufus to go with you and Alexander to Jerusalem as they both have to learn the ways of men from their wise father as they grow up. Simon, I will be fine here, preparing for your return. I know the Lord will protect you all today as you make your journey to Jerusalem."

Simon turned to Bayla and kissed her softly. Then he moved his hand in the air, signaling Rufus to come with them, and said, "Rufus, yes, you can go with me and Alexander to Jerusalem to observe the first day of Passover. I know you will learn many things, but take it all as a way of knowing the ways of the Lord."

The look of disappointment on Rufus' face changed to admiration as his eyes lit up with joy and excitement. While Simon admired Rufus, Alexander continued looking at people walking inside Jerusalem.

Rufus celebrated, "Thank you, Father! I am so excited." He then turned to Alexander and said, "Alexander, Father says I can go with you to Jerusalem to observe the first day of Passover! Yea!!"

"Alright, Rufus, you will have to calm down. We still have to walk and prepare for our journey to the city today. I hope you are up for the journey, little brother." Alexander tried to ease his little brother's excitement.

Bayla addressed Alexander and explained to him, "Alright, Alexander, you will have to be on your best behavior and watch out for your brother Rufus while your father may be busy on the market today. It is a busy place, so make sure you two stay together. No running off for any adventure, boys, okay?"

Alexander reassured his mother, "Yes, Mother, I will take care of Rufus and keep an eye on Father as well. I am sure he will show me many things today."

Rufus' excitement was nowhere to be toned down, as he was really happy that he was going with his father and brother for the first time. So, he turned to his mother and said, "Mother, I know I will have so much to tell you when I return. I can't wait to see the city today!"

"Patience, Alexander and Rufus, we will see the city soon enough. I am sure we will all have a very good time in the city of Jerusalem today." Simon reassured his sons, and then he looked at Bayla and questioned, "My love, are you sure you will be alright by yourself here all day?"

Bayla said, "Simon, my love, God has, and God will take care of us all. The Lord has been good to us, and I will be fine preparing for your return to celebrate the feast of Passover with my great men of valor."

Simon embraced his wife once again, and Rufus and Alexander hugged their mother while Alexander said, "Okay, Mother, we have all we need now. I will see you later tonight."

"Bayla, I thank you for packing us a day's meal and providing water for us. I am indeed blessed that you are in my life. You are truly my gift from God." Simon was grateful to his wife for thinking about them more than they did.

Bayla answered lovingly, "My love, you are all the Lord has provided for me to take care of. You and our sons are my life, and I will always take care of you, Simon."

Rufus called out to his mother once again before stepping out and saying, "Mother, I love you. I will tell you about my adventures in Jerusalem tonight!"

And so, Simon, Rufus, and Alexander started their journey as they stepped out of the house just outside the city of Jerusalem. They began the journey to observe the Passover festivities in Jerusalem and shop at the market there.

They walked for about twenty miles in the countryside with their carts, supplies, and merchandise to exchange and purchase stuff they needed at the market. While they were making their way inside the city, they couldn't help but notice a crowd streaming from the city of Jerusalem toward Golgotha.

As Simon and his sons walked toward the city of Jerusalem, they noticed that men, women, and Roman soldiers were lining up on the road and that the crowd was growing. Simon felt strange about everything happening in the city but continued his trek. At the same time, Alexander and Rufus stayed behind their father, taking care of the camels and the market's supplies.

As they kept walking, Alexander again questioned, "Father, what is going on today? Is this a part of the Passover festivities you told us about?"

Even though Simon had no idea what was happening, he was now sure that it was not a part of the Passover. And he replied, "No, my son, this is something different, and I am not sure what to make of this that we are seeing but do stay close to me since I see Roman soldiers, Pharisees, and leaders of the city gathering from Jerusalem right now."

As they walked and talked, Alexander found his answers to his questions. Jesus suddenly came on the road leading out of Jerusalem, carrying a cross. He wore a crown of thorns on his head, and blood was streaming from his body. The only thing Alexander and Rufus could notice about this man was his brown skin, curly woolly hair that reached his shoulders, and a lot of discomfort in his brown eyes.

His steps were shaky and unstable as he attempted to bear the Cross on his back as he moved on Golgotha Road, leaving from the city of Jerusalem. Blood was dripping behind Jesus with every step, and suddenly, with the weight of the Cross pressing on his back, he trembled and fell, dropping the Cross.

Instead of helping him to get up, a Roman Soldier took a whip and slashed at Jesus. The sound was devastating and terrorizing to hear and it shook Simon and his two sons.

Simon, when he tried to look closely, observed that Jesus' robs was covered in blood and sweat as he was lying on the street after he fell. It was obvious that Jesus was exhausted, and when he further tried to stand, his steps stumbled again due to his pain.

While all this was happening, Simon kept walking a few feet ahead of his sons.

As Jesus struggled to get up, the Roman soldier and Simon caught each other's eyes, and the soldier called out to Simon and said, "You there! Get this Cross up and help him carry it up this hill! This man will be crucified today, and I need you to help him and carry this Cross! Let's go; we must make haste now!"

The Roman soldier slashed his whip, and Simon looked back at his sons Alexander and Rufus. Fear and terror were visible in their eyes as they saw their father being picked out from the crowd to carry the Cross of Jesus.

Simon was also terrified by this, but he told his sons to remain where they were out of concern that they would be detained for obstructing the Roman soldier.

Alexander couldn't help but ask his father in distress, "Father! What would you have us do?"

Rufus also called out in fear, "Father! Please don't let them take you away." He then turned to one of the soldiers standing nearby and said to him, "Please don't kill our father!"

Simon looked at Alexander and instructed, "Alexander! Watch over Rufus; do not approach this Roman soldier. I have to obey his orders. Make sure you stay here! Do not be afraid, my sons. The Lord will protect us! Stay here and watch for my return!"

As Simon attempted to lift the Cross, his steps felt tentative. For the first time, he was so near Jesus that he could see his suffering. He was much more frightened when he saw Jesus beaten to death and covered in his blood.

Another aspect that worried Simon was the fact that he knew his sons were with him, and he was terrified that the crucifixion could be his own fate if he refused to obey the Roman soldiers. And it was something he didn't want in his life. Even though he was hesitant to carry the Cross for Jesus, Simon still agreed for his family's sake and went ahead with Jesus on his journey without knowing who Jesus was.

Simon saw Jesus and noticed how bloody and lethargic he was. He felt great terror and sympathy for Jesus, who was exhausted and had a bloody body looking close to death. Simon picked up Jesus, stabilized his Cross on his shoulders, and helped Jesus walk with the Cross, which was very heavy.

Simon whispered, "Lord, give me the strength to bear this heavy Cross on this hill. Protect my sons; protect us all, Lord.

Simon was hesitant to be a part of this act, but as Jesus' blood and sweat touched Simon, it gave him courage and strength. Jesus looked at Simon, smiled, and prayed for his strength to bear the heavy Cross up Golgotha's hill with Jesus leaning on Simon's shoulders.

Simon did not know Jesus was the Son of God. But Simon felt peace and strength while being in the direct presence of Jesus and helping him carry the Cross.

Alexander and Rufus were down the hill, terrified by seeing their father carrying the massive Cross on his shoulder.

Alexander shouted in fear, "Father, please do not fall!"

Simon stumbled on the rugged pavement up Golgatha's hill, where Jesus was to be crucified. The weight of the Cross and Jesus was quite heavy on Simon. Simon's face quaked from the pain of the Cross on his back. But just then, Jesus' hands touched Simon's back, and suddenly Simon felt better, and his anguish left him as he carried the Cross for Jesus.

The crowd was crying and shouting, looking at Simon and Jesus. Some shouted hateful words while others were praying and meditating, knowing about who Jesus was.

At last, the two men reached Calvary, where Jesus was to be nailed to the Cross. There was a hole dug in the ground where the Cross was to be erected after nailing Jesus onto it.

As soon as they reached the place, a Roman soldier slashed his whip and ordered Simon to get away from the presence of Jesus.

Simon was covered in Jesus' blood, and apart from being terrified at first, he felt like a new person, and his spirit and life's focus were not the same anymore.

As he moved away from Jesus, Simon kneeled to the ground and prayed to God again, "Lord, please bless this man, for his presence upon me was one of peace and blessings. God, let this moment in my life be my point of renewing my mission to serve you, Lord. Thank you for sparing me and my sons this merciless danger of death today!"

When they saw their father stumbling to the ground, Rufus and Alexander ran up and grabbed Simon. The blood of Jesus was upon him, and this sight terrified them.

Rufus asked with concern and terror, "Father, are you alright? Are you hurt, Father?"

Simon replied, not knowing that he helped fulfill one of the prophecies, "No, my son, the Lord has given me strength and blessed me this day to help this innocent man to the place of crucifixion. This was God's servant and a man that was special to all humankind."

Simon, Rufus, and Alexander observed the nails being driven through the hands and feet of Jesus to the Cross in preparation to be crucified before all the citizens of Jerusalem.

Jesus' blood dripped from the Cross as he quenched and responded to the pain and agony as the nails were driven through his wrist and his feet.

Without moving his gaze from Jesus, Alexander asked, "Father, who is that man, and what did he do, Father?"

Simon looked at him, then back to Jesus, and replied, "His name is Jesus!"

Simon paused and continued, "Alexander, many say he was a prophet or a spiritual leader. I can say now that he is a divine man of God, an innocent man who is being put to death for what he believed. God has placed truth in him to bring to his people.

Tears streamed down from Simon's eyes as he spoke to his sons. As they were talking, the Roman soldiers erected the Cross of Jesus vertically, adding to his pain and suffering even more.

As soon as the Cross was erected, the sky turned gray, and the ground shook below the feet of Simon and his sons. The view was harrowing, and Simon had no words to explain his feelings. Even though he didn't know Jesus, he still felt excruciating pain in his heart.

Around the ninth hour of Jesus's crucifixion, he died on the Cross. The earth shook as the lightning and thunder sound cracked the ground. The sky darkened even more, and a mist of rain fell to the ground. The veil of holiness was torn from top to bottom.

After Jesus was dead, one of the Roman soldiers pierced Jesus on the sides, and a stream of blood and water came out of his body.

Looking at this sight, Simon and his sons hugged each other with tears in their eyes. Simon once again looked at his body and clothes that were covered in Jesus's blood and felt blessed.

As it all ended, Simon and his sons began to walk away from the standing Cross. Two of Jesus' disciples approached Simon and his sons as they walked only a few steps. One went by the name Mark, and the other was known as John.

Simon could tell from the torn expressions on their faces that they were close to Jesus Christ.

As they approached Simon, Mark said, "Hey, what are your and your son's names? My name is Mark, and I follow Jesus and his teachings. I am honored for what you did for Jesus today by carrying his Cross. Where are you from?"

Before Simon could reply, John added, "I am so thankful you were here to carry the Cross for Jesus Christ, our Lord. He was our spiritual leader, and I feel that he has had a significant impact on you. Jesus has that effect on all people that he blesses with his message of redemption.

I know you will never be the same, Simon. Neither you nor your sons will forget this day that you helped carry the Cross of the Savior of the World, Jesus, the Son of God."

Simon replied, still trying to recover from what he witnessed, "My name is Simon, and these are my sons Alexander and Rufus. We are from Cyrene and live in Rome. We have traveled to Jerusalem to observe Passover today.

Simon took a pause and questioned, "Who was this Jesus? I felt his presence and divine power as he prayed for my strength today. I have never felt this way before. It was as if he knew me and my entire life. His presence burns in my heart."

Mark replied, "Yes, Jesus is the son of God, and he was our leader and Lord. Before this happened, Jesus said, 'I will lay down my life; no one has power over my life; I give my life freely; but in three days, I will pick it back up again with all power in my hands.'

I believe every word that has ever come out of his mouth. But today, he is dead. All of my brothers are praying in hiding as they are afraid of what is about to come as the Roman soldiers are seeking to kill anyone who says and professes that Jesus was the Lord.

Mark paused, looked at Simon's sons, and then said, "We will keep your sons Rufus and Alexander in our prayers, Simon of Cyrene, as you return to Rome. Remember what you see here, Simon.

Mark and John had tears in their eyes while conversing with Simon. As they were done, Simon hugged both of them for their prayer. Simon could feel the love that John and Mark had for Jesus. Both men turned around as they, along with Alexander and Rufus, watched the body of Jesus Christ being lowered down from the Cross. The disciples lowered their heads in Jesus's glory and might while tears streamed down their cheeks.

Simon and his sons returned home as devout Christians and determined to be great missionaries of the Gospel of Jesus Christ in Antioch, Rome. Meanwhile, the disciples, John and Mark, returned to Jerusalem.

As soon as Simon and his two sons returned to the place of rest, Bayla looked at Simon's condition and was concerned about what had happened to him. She questioned in a panicky tone, "My lord, Simon, what happened to you, my love? Where are your wounds? What is all this blood on you, Simon?

Then she turned to her sons and inquired from them, "Alexander, Rufus, what happened to your father? I must know what occurred in Jerusalem today!

She again turned to Simon and said, I am so thankful that the Lord protected you, Simon, and my sons! Praise the Lord for your safe return, my love, and for my sons. Oh, lay down, Simon, please lay down."

Bayla had no idea that the blood Simon was covered in was not his own but was the holy blood of Jesus Christ.

Simon calmed her down and said, "My love, this is not my blood. I had to help a spiritual leader by the name of Jesus carry his Cross and help him up Calvary Hill toward his crucifixion. He prayed for me, and I felt protected and strengthened tonight. My life will never be the same, my love."

CHAPTER 2

The Challenge of Power

After getting cleaned up, Simon lit a fire, and the entire family gathered around him. Bayla brought Simon food and also gave it to her sons as the Passover feast began.

While eating, Simon explained everything that occurred in the morning, and everyone looked at him with curiosity as they wanted to know and reflect on what was happening.

Bayla, as she didn't witness any of those events happening from her eyes, embraced Simon as he was shaken while reflecting on the events of the crucifixion.

While Simon was talking, Rufus interrupted and said, "Mother, I was so scared, but I prayed for Father as he was forced to carry Jesus' Cross to the top of the hill. I felt sad, but when I saw Father walk back to me and hug me, I felt safe and wonderful."

Alexander added, "The day was not what I expected, Mother. It was the man that you said was Jesus who had been crucified. He was so bloody and beaten that I was terrified when Father had to help carry his Cross. I am glad Father had the strength to carry such a big cross and help Jesus."

With love, Simon patted Alexander's head and replied, "Yes, my sons, we will never be the same, and we will continue to share God's word with all who will hear it."

He then addressed Bayla and informed her, "Bayla, I met John and Mark today, who were followers of Jesus. They told me that Jesus was the Savior and said he would die, but on the third day, he would also rise again from the dead. After meeting Jesus today and seeing all I have seen, I believe he is the Messiah, the son of God."

"You are my Lord and Priest of our home, and where you are, Simon, we will also be my love. I will serve the Lord and be your helpmate as you complete your mission to spread the word of the Lord." Bayla smiled and assured Simon she would be his companion and supporter forever. The family hugged and embraced each other as they knew that the love of Jesus Christ has touched their lives.

Time passed, and Simon continued to preach and spread the word of the Lord all over Rome and converted many non-believers to Christianity. Alexander and Rufus also grew up and had wives and sons by then. Apart from being involved in their familial lives, Alexander and Rufus were missionaries in Antioch, Rome. God used them to perform miracles by healing the sick and raising the dead by touching them.

One day, the family greeted the Apostle Paul as he traveled throughout Rome in Antioch, performing miracles and preaching the Gospel of Jesus Christ.

Simon greeted Paul as he entered their house: "Greetings, Paul, I am honored to greet you in the name of our Lord Jesus Christ. You are most welcome here in Antioch, Rome. Please make yourself at home. Meet my wife Bayla and my sons Alexander and Rufus."

Paul replied, "Thank you, Simon, for your great hospitality, and I see that the grace of God is with you here in Rome."

Paul was a middle-aged man with less curly hair and a light olive-brown skin color. They knew each other from the time Simon and Paul started preaching. This was Paul's first visit to Antioch, so it was important for Simon to introduce Paul to the other Christians there. So, the other day, Simon took Apostle Paul to the Antioch church assembly in Rome and said, "It would be an honor, Paul, to have you speak to the believers of Jesus Christ here in Antioch, Rome. We are eager to hear of your wisdom and the message we have heard so much about as you travel throughout Rome."

Apostle Paul smiled and began preaching, "Grace to you and peace from God our Father and the Lord Jesus Christ. Firstly, I thank

God for you all. I longed to see you so that I may impart some spiritual gift to make you strong, namely that you and I may be mutually encouraged by each other's faith. I do not want you to be unaware, brothers, that I planned many times to come to you but have been prevented from doing so until now so that I might have a harvest among you, just as I have had among the gentlemen. I am obligated both to Greeks and non-Greeks, both to the wise and the foolish.

That is why I am so eager to preach the Gospel to you who are in Rome. I am not ashamed of the Gospel because it is the power of God for the salvation of everyone who believes, first for the Jew, then for the Gentile. For in the Gospel, the righteousness from God is revealed, a righteousness that is by faith from first to last, just as it is written: the righteous and just will live by faith."

Apostle Paul ended his speech while Simon came to him to express his admiration and gratitude. He hugged Paul as the crowd cheered for his words and understanding of God.

Simon aimed to live by devoting their lives to preaching and spreading the message of the Lord and bringing back as many people to the righteous path. However, Simon and his sons could not do it smoothly. The government of Jerusalem started to kill Christians, disciples, and the priests of Jesus Christ. They imprisoned the faithful of Jesus' disciples and the early church leaders. The nearest disciple of Jesus, Mark, who met Simon on the day of the crucifixion, had been murdered, and the government imprisoned John. They were now searching for a chance to put their hands on the Apostle Paul.

CHAPTER 3

The Militant and Powerful Protectors of the Sworn Sacred Oath of Simon

God's blessings were with Simon and his family, as there was a special priesthood called Zebulon. The High Priest from Ethiopia arrived in Rome. His purpose was to investigate and ask about the power of Simon and his sons. They also wanted to protect Simon. To them, the gift of the power of God should be protected from the world.

The Priest met with Simon and discussed the protection of his family, to which Simson said, "I love serving the people of God and building churches to spread God's word. I have witnessed the crucifixion of Christ, felt his blood bless me, and even felt him pray for me. He even rose from the dead on the third day. I will serve him until I die."

Zebulon urged, "Simon, the disciples of Jesus are being killed and murdered by those who want to keep power in the hands of the government of Jerusalem. Please consider protecting your sons and their children from the same destruction as many disciples. I also love Jesus' teachings, but I want to see you live and keep your power of God's healing. You had contact with the risen Savior, Jesus himself. Please let us protect you."

Simon did not fear those killing and imprisoning the disciples; he said, "No matter where we go or what we do, Zebulon, people will love and hate us. I thank you for wanting to protect us and keep us within the confines of the church walls, but I am a man of the people, and God has protected me over my life. When it is my time, I will die as a servant of the Lord."

Zebulon knew the importance of Simon and his family; he tried to convince him, "I will assign a protective priesthood to protect your family, and these priests will live around you and protect your children and grandchildren. These priests will be holy men who will serve as a special guard in your family."

Simon thought about his family and grandchildren, whom he loved a lot. He said, "I agree to this protection for my family, children, and grandchildren. I know I am old and was blessed to serve the living savior, Jesus Christ. I will be among the people in Rome until I complete my work to build the church here in Antioch. All my sons and daughters for many generations should be protected and even placed in a place of refuge if the wicked government will even try to kill them or imprison them. Do I have your word, Zebulon?"

Zebulon reassured, "Yes, Simon, you are a true man of God and one that was blessed directly by Jesus Christ himself. I will establish an order in our priesthood to protect and serve your family for all generations. Your seed will be protected and watched over by our priesthood."

Zebulon embraced Simon, promising to assign security guards for him and his family. The special Priesthood left. On the other hand, Simon knew that he was getting older and that his family should be protected from the cruel government of Jerusalem.

After the meeting with Zebulon, Simon lived for only a few days; he already knew that his time was coming and would soon leave the mortal plane. He was satisfied with his life, as he considered himself blessed to be chosen to help Jesus on the day of his crucifixion. It was his funeral when his family was there to pay respect to him.

***

After his death, his sons continued to build churches, preach to believers and non-believers, and spread the message of God. Time passed, many wars happened, eras to eras, and the world kept developing.

It was now the post-modern era of 2015, and almost everything had changed, but the Zebulun Priesthood had remembered their promise to protect Simon's family. The only difference was that the modern-day family of Simon was not aware that the Priesthood, which Zebulun started in the era of Jesus Christ, was protecting them.

In 2015, Courtney, an 18-year-old African-American girl, was right in the thick of it all. She was well-liked, easy to talk to, and undeniably attractive. Despite these qualities, there was a restlessness within her; she was on a quest to uncover her true purpose in life. Coming from a middle-class background, she was no stranger to the value of hard work and was looking for opportunities to earn extra money and make her mark.

One day, she was reading a book in a library. After a while, she closed the book and addressed her friends gathered around her: "Hey, what are you guys doing today? I am supposed to be going to biology class today. I have an exam this Friday, so I have to study. What's going on?"

One of her friends, Tamara, said, "Girl, you have been in here all morning, Courtney. You will ace that test anyway; you always do, girl. But if you are going to get to biology class, you better hurry up because it starts in about 5 minutes, so you better get going."

Her other friend Candace said, "Hey, Courtney, will you be busy later? We will hang out later on campus for the student rally this afternoon. We should meet there, alright?"

Courtney thought about her schedule and replied, "Well, I will have to see. I may have to work in the lab today, but if I complete my assignment early, I can catch up with you guys then, all right."

Tamara humorously told Courtney, "All right, girl, don't let your head explode with all that studying you do. By the way, you better hurry to class; you know you don't want to be late today."

Courtney gathered her books and rushed to her biology class from the library. She remembered something and returned to speak to Tamara and Candace before running out the library doors to class.

She said, "Hey, if you guys are going to that rally on campus, I want to go too. Just text me where you guys will be, and I will meet you there. Okay, got to go. Catch up to you later."

Her friend Candace replied, "Okay, I will text you the location where we will be at the rally on campus; see you later, Courtney."

Courtney was in a hurry; she did not want to miss her biology class, so she rushed across the campus with her books. She was trying to get to her class as quickly as she could. Suddenly, out of a hurry, she ran into a priest she did not notice. The Father was knocked to the ground. Thankfully, he was not hurt; Courtney froze. She had no idea she would pop into a priest; she returned to the zone and gave him a hand.

She said worriedly, "Oh my God! I am so sorry, Father. Please forgive me. I did not see you there. Are you alright?

Let me help you up. I am a Christian; please don't hold this against me today for accidentally running into you."

The Priest, Abaracus, got up and replied, "It's all right, my child; I am sure it was my fault as well. I am fine, just a little off my feet, but I will be fine. I don't think God will punish you for accidentally knocking over a priest on your way to class. I am fine, thank you. Are you okay?"

Courtney responded to him in a rush, "I am all right; nothing hurts at all. Thank you, Father. Take care. God bless, and I do apologize again."

Abaracus, was an African Priest. He was the descendant of the Ethiopian Priesthood that Zebulon started. He was commissioned to oversee the lives of Courtney and her family. However, Courtney was unaware of his existence or the sacred Priesthood that watched her family.

However, as Courtney was running late, she rushed into her lab, and as soon as she entered, she received a text from Tamara and Candace reminding her about the rally. Courtney read the text, looked around the lab, and kept her phone away as she still had time and had other things to finish.

Courtney then completed her work, and once she was done, she put away the specimen she was working on in the glass science cabinet. After that, she removed her goggles, closed the cabinet, washed her hands, and grabbed her book bag to leave the lab.

The entire time she traveled from her lab to the rally, her mind flickered between what the rally would be about. She was excited, but she was also unsure whether this rally would benefit her or be a waste of time.

Courtney arrived at the rally and met Tamara and Candace as they greeted her. Then, they sat on bleachers to hear the message about the mission to give blood to the Save a Life campaign and how students could also earn money by donating blood. It was exciting, as they were all looking for ways to make extra money. In addition to that, Courtney was always ready to help those in need. The idea "to love your neighbors as yourself" was instilled in Courtney since she was just a little girl. So, it was obvious that donating blood and the chance of making extra money out of it would be a great plan for the night, for Courtney and her friends.

The rally, no doubt, was very informative and full of music. It also included testimonials of how people have been impacted by the latest research with new scientific breakthroughs in stem cells and technology to enhance function for renewing human tissue.

While enjoying the rally, Candace said, "Hey girl, this rally is nice. I knew you would like it too. Tamara thought you would be interested, especially when it came to science and technology."

Before Courtney could reply, Tamara interrupted, "You like it, girl! This is so your thing. With all that stem cell research and the ability to donate blood and help give life to others. I knew you would be interested in this campaign on campus today."

Courtney looked around once and responded, "Wow, it is very exciting for sure! I am planning to give some blood to help someone out and help with the research of helping others. I like that they pay you as well."

"Yeah! That's a cool way to earn some gas money and some hangout money, especially when you don't have to do anything but sit there and donate some blood." Candace said it with a smirk.

Tamara interrupted again and said, "Besides, girl, I know you like helping people, so here is your shot to do just that and get some money, and you don't even have to get a job to do this. Thank God!"

Tamara scoffed and continued, "I don't have time to work any other student job on campus this semester."

"You know that is right. I was looking for a way to help some people and do something meaningful in my life right now. Thanks, guys, for telling me about this life-giving science rally today. I think I will donate some blood, too. I am interested; just let me know when you guys go, and we can go together." Courtney was thankful to them.

They all enjoyed the rally together, and as it ended, Courtney, Tamara, and Candace left and went their separate ways. They were all happy and contended that they found out about this rally and came here. It was a great event that they all enjoyed together.

CHAPTER 4

The Blood Of The Innocent

The other morning was just another usual day for Courtney, as she was home with her family. After she finished her morning routine, Courtney entered the kitchen where her mom was. As soon as she saw her mom, she greeted her.

"Good morning, Mom!" Courtney said it with a smile.

And her mother replied, "Good morning, love!"

Courtney's mother, Zephora Malveaux, was of African-American/Indian descent, was around 38, and had a biracial complexion that made her stand out in public. By profession, Zephora was an optometrist, meaning she was a healthcare professional concerned with examining eyes for vision defects and diagnosing and treating such conditions. Despite her professional emergencies, Courtney and her mother were quite close and had a warm relationship like any other mother-daughter relationship.

On the other hand, Courtney's father, Marcus Malveaux, was an African-American and was somewhat around the age of 42. He was a tall and handsome pharmacist, which meant that, just like Zephora, Marcus was always surrounded by work.

But his work responsibilities never shadowed Marcus to ignore his familial duties. He managed both his house and work pretty well. Additionally, Marcus was very protective and close to Courtney, as they shared a very close bond.

Marcus was a descendant of the Simon family line, and the blessings of the power of God have been traced throughout his family. However, the power had been suppressed to the point that Marcus had never fully embraced the family blessing since his generation had never explored it. Instead, it was only apparent to the selected births throughout the centuries that God selected to express the power and use the blessing given to the seed of Simon. Even though Marcus was aware of the legacy of his vague family history, he only thought about it as folklore and a fantasy.

Just like her father, Courtney knew nothing of her family's sacred blessings, but little did she know that she will soon discover this blessing as she was about to witness the calling of God in her life.

Right after greeting her mom, Courtney asked, "Mom, has Dad come home yet?"

Zephora studied Courtney's facial expressions and understood she was excited about something. And so, instead of just replying to her question, she inquired, "Hey sweetheart, what are you up to? You look like you have some great news to tell me about. What's up? And no, your father has not come home yet, but he should be coming in a little bit."

Instead of answering her questions, Courtney took a deep breath, inhaling the delicious aroma permeating the kitchen. Courtney mentioned, "You know, that food smells good, Mom. What are you cooking tonight?"

Zephora smiled and answered, "I am preparing some great parmesan chicken. Your father wanted me to cook it for us tonight. But don't try to get out of what is asked, sweetheart. What do you have going on these days at college?"

As Zephora asked Courtney for the second time, she had no other option but to answer her mother, so she said, "Well, I am always trying to discover what I am supposed to do with my life, Mom. I often feel I have a higher purpose, but I don't quite know what it is."

"Well, sweetheart, that is why you are in college." Zephora paused to check the food in the oven and continued, "So you can look around and see what you like about your interests and what you want to pursue as a career. I know you like science and healthcare, so allow yourself to explore those areas and see what appeals to you."

Courtney said, "You know, you and Dad have great careers, and I admire both of you guys in what you do. I hope I can be as successful and happy as you guys are one day."

Zephora looked at Courtney with compassion and motioned for Courtney to come to her. She embraced her daughter and said, "Hey Courtney, baby, you can do whatever you like in your life. Your Father and I both are extremely proud of you and always have been. We believe in you and your life choices. You have always found a way to do the right thing, baby. I know that you will do just that now as you pursue your life goals for the future. You are special, Courtney. You are my blessed child who has always made me smile. God has his hands on you. Trust what is in your heart, and God will lead you to what is best for you, Courtney."

Zephora's words of appreciation worked, and Courtney replied, "Mom, you always know how to calm me down and help me focus and feel confident about my life. When did you know that being an optometrist was what you wanted to be in your career?"

Zephora felt nostalgic at this question as she recalled when she first decided what she wanted to be. "Well, baby, I knew I wanted to be an optometrist when I went to an optometrist as a kid, and the doctor placed an eye spectrum on my eyes and helped me see clearly. I remember finally being able to see so many things, and I never forgot about that experience. It was then I knew I wanted to do as I learned more about the field. I was hooked, baby."

Amazed by her mother's response, Courtney replied, "Wow, I feel that way about medicine and helping people with advancing technology in health care, Mom. I am excited about seeing people live healthier and have a better opportunity to heal and get better from all types of diseases."

Zephora exclaimed, "Hey, that is it, Courtney. If that is where your heart is, baby, you must pursue that passion. You are great at that. I knew you were brilliant when you got your scholarships, and you have always done great in school your whole life, baby. You can do medicine as a physician or even as a medical scientist, baby."

As Zephora expressed her excitement about Courtney's passion for science and helping others, Courtney felt relieved. As she talked to her mom, she realized that her life mission was always in front of her. It was just that she needed someone to validate it for her.

Courtney enthusiastically looked at her mother and replied, "You know that excites me, Mom. I attended a science rally today on the college campus that promoted donating blood and giving life to people who needed blood to live. It was amazing to see how the blood plasma and transfusions helped so many people, according to the testimonials at the rally. Tamara and Candace were excited, and I wanted to donate to help people who need the blood to give life to someone else. They pay as well. I like that!"

Zephora replied, "Well, it seems you have a unique way to help mankind, baby. I applaud all of you guys for wanting to donate blood; it is truly a great thing to help those who will need a blood transfusion to save lives, baby girl." Zephora paused and then continued, "There you go. I knew you would be thinking of doing something very special in your life. Wow, you get paid too. Hey, I am sure you guys like that a lot. It sounds like gas money to me, Courtney, and you are helping people, too. Superfriends to the rescue."

As soon as Zephora said this, she and Courtney began to laugh together, and in the meantime, dinner was also almost ready.

As the mother and daughter enjoyed their moment, Marcus entered the house and noticed the smell of Parmesan chicken. He felt upbeat and warm due to the aroma that filled the atmosphere of the entire house. He went straight into the kitchen and greeted Courtney and Zephora, who were still busy talking and laughing.

As soon as they noticed that Marcus was there, Zephora greeted him with a kiss, and Courtney hugged her father.

Marcus couldn't resist asking, "Hey baby, I'm home, ooh wee. Something smells good up in here, for real!" Then he noticed the food already served on the table, complimented Zephora, and said, "Awe baby, you made the Parmesan chicken tonight. Oh, that is the best stuff, for real. Honey, thank you for cooking what I wanted tonight. I hope you had a great day at the office."

Before Zephora could answer, Courtney interrupted and asked, "Hey, Daddy! How was your day? I am sure you were busy filling all those prescriptions today."

Marcus replied, "Oh yeah, baby girl, Daddy is on the job for real, so what's up with you, and how are you doing in your studies, baby? It is great to have your home tonight."

Before Courtney could answer this time, Zephora interrupted and told Marcus about whatever they were talking about before he walked in. She said, "Marcus, Courtney was just telling me how she wants to go into the medical field and do something to better mankind, baby. She is excited about donating blood at the college blood drive sometime next week. Baby, you remember you used to donate blood to get some money, too?"

Marcus looked at Courtney with pride and said to her, "Well, baby, I am always proud of you. Your mother and I always knew you would be something special. I can't wait to see Courtney as Dr. Malveaux."

Marcus paused to imagine something in his head and continued, "Oh, wee baby girl, that sounds good to me. I will be your first patient. I am sure your Momma and I will need some medical attention at that time in our old age, especially your mother."

Marcus joked, and everyone laughed. Then Zephora said, "Alright, Marcus, you got jokes, right?" She then addressed Courtney and said, "Courtney, your dad is the one who is the old man around here. If anybody needs medical assistance, it will be him. He should know better than to try to clown me."

Everyone laughed once again and enjoyed the moment. After some time, they all sat at the table and prepared to say grace.

Before they said the grace, Courtney looked at her father and said, "Daddy, I am glad you and Mom are supportive of me pursuing a medical career and even donating blood to help people. I learned that donating can impact society and help give life to people. I feel that this is a way for me to be a blessing to people, which is a great gift of life from me, and I get paid to do it, too."

Marcus appreciated her and replied, "Courtney, that is a great idea. I always knew that you had a great heart, baby. God is certainly giving you a great purpose for your life. Just keep looking and listening to what you feel in your heart, and your life choices will be open. Your mother and I have been blessed in the healthcare profession, and I know you will be, too. I think helping others is a great thing, baby."

Courtney looked at her father with love and said, "I love you, Daddy. I love you too, Momma. You guys are always the best. Well, Daddy, do you want to bless the food tonight?"

Zephora joked, "Well, someone has to bless the food now because I am getting hungry now."

Marcus smiled and said, "Alright, I will bless the food. Lord, bless this food and let it be a blessing to us all. Thank you for blessing Courtney as she is guided by your wisdom, Lord, and thank you for blessing Zephora to make this wonderful meal tonight, amen."

Then, the family began to eat the food and enjoy conversation.

CHAPTER 5

The Miraculous Events of Modern Times even with Abandoned Disbelief

The next morning, the girls reached the blood donation center and stood in line. While standing in the line, waiting for their turn to donate blood, the girls filled out the necessary consent forms.

After sufficient time had lapsed, a nurse finally approached the girls. She placed the instrument on their arms to mark where the blood would be extracted. She then proceeded to clean the marked spot with alcohol to make it sterile. She then injected a needle to extract the blood from their arms and direct it to a bag. As the blood left Courtney's body, a series of unfortunate events start to occur simultaneously across the town.

The day had a tinge of unexpected horror vibe to it. Nothing out of the ordinary; these were just life-threatening situations for people from all walks of life.

Death and tragedy struck an Asian family. A mother, young son, and father were driving a car on the freeway when the course of their day changed drastically. The three were having a random teen-whisk the events of their day when suddenly, an eighteen-wheeler lost control. The truck driver was driving peacefully when a deer appeared on the road. To save the deer, the truck driver steered the truck in another direction and drove straight into the car with the Asian family.

The mother was already accelerating the car. The boy was in the passenger seat, and his sister was in the backseat. The car had reached a speed of 58 miles per hour when it got breached with impact. The mother lost control as the car crossed the beam and went off the road. The car crash landed upon rails, which broke the windows. The mother was compressed between her seat and the steering wheel. She broke her ribs and legs and ruptured her lung, which caused internal bleeding in her abdominal tissue.

The son's face was cut in various places by the glass. The daughter got ejected out of the windshield and landed in a pool of her own blood. She fractured her skull and femur. She lay on the ground unconscious, suffering from internal bleeding, too.

When the boy gained consciousness and saw the aftermath, he screamed. The truck driver freaked out, and he called 911. He was terrified beyond anything. Eventually, the police cars could be seen, and ambulance sirens could be heard.

At the same time, in another part of the town, a fire was erupting on the rooftop of a building. A white male fireman was trying to extinguish the fire when he heard someone scream below, "I think it's gonna blow. Get out of there now!"

An explosion occurred. The fireman fell into the burning building and was taken away by the loud, massive burning fire. He was unconscious as over 60% of his body got burned. He got blind in one eye, and his facial skin melted away to the tissues and muscles. His chest and arms were all raw and red, with blisters and burnt muscles covering his abdominal area.

The metal pieces in the explosion acted as missiles and pierced his chest, all the way to his lungs and spleen, causing massive internal bleeding. As he was rescued, all the rescuers were shocked and horrified at the sight. They quickly transferred him to a trauma unit.

Similarly, a blood transfusion was taking place at a hospital for a child with leukemia. The child's blood started to clot, and she started shaking. She was having difficulty breathing. All the nurses and the child's mother began to panic and scream as they had no idea what to do next.

And finally, at another end of the town, a group of African-American kids were in a standoff with a gang over a property dispute matter. A guy from the opposite gang threw an insult, which led to a fight. Everyone started to throw hands. One member of the gang pulls out his gun and took a shot. He missed who he was supposed to shoot, and instead, shot his friend. The friend stumbled to the ground, screaming and gasping for breath.

Everyone else was terrified at seeing so much blood leaving his body. Someone called the police, while the others fled away. The sound of the gunshot hung in the air until the paramedics and police arrived. The one who was shot was hurriedly taken to the hospital.

All of this was happening while Courtney was donating her blood. She was completely oblivious to all of these events happening. She focused on the show she was watching on her tablet as she laid back on the chair and donated blood.

Courtney became curious about her blood donation and asked the nurse, "I wonder how many people can be helped with just one pint of my blood."

The nurse replied, "I know that one pint of blood can help save at least four people and help keep them alive if they need the blood to save their lives. You have truly done a great thing today."

This made Courtney feel good. She was happy. The nurse resumed speaking,

"Alright, now you guys rest up and have a cookie and some juice or water on your way out. Keep the bandage on your arm for a few hours to allow the area to stay clean from where the blood was drawn." The nurse said with a smile after she pulled the needle out of Courtney's hand. She then wrapped the bandage on her arm. After a while, all the girls left the building and went home.

***

Soon after, the fireman was taken to the same hospital where Courtney and her friends donated blood. He had to be treated instantly, because he was very seriously injured and needed help. His burns needed to be taken care of as soon as possible. Therefore, he was taken to the ICU. Tubes and IV drips were injected into his right and left arms, with an oxygen mask placed over his mouth to let him breathe while his vitals and scans were checked.

The doctors suggested that as the firefighter already lost a lot of blood, he needed a blood transfusion. Luckily, after checking, doctors discovered that Courtney's blood was a match. Coincidently, just as the blood transfusion took place, all of his burns started to heal. His eye began to twitch, and a new tissue layer was forming over it as well. The ECG monitor noted an elevated heartbeat, and his blood pressure stabilized.

The fireman gained consciousness and opened his eyes. He woke up in shock and terror. He still thought he was trapped inside that building and was still being burned alive as the last thing he remembered was the roof collapsing.

A nurse hurried to see the fuss. She screamed at the sight of the obvious healing. "How did he heal so quickly? What was this miracle?" The nurse said to herself, then screamed and called a doctor. The doctor was terrified of this miracle as well. A team of nurses gathered around the fireman and sedated him so that he could calm down.

The doctor instructed a nurse, "I need 20mg versed IV stat in this patient now!" He then stepped back and asked another nurse, "What happened? Did you see how this miraculous event took place?"

The nurse replied, "I came in, and the patient was in shock, screaming and obviously stunned himself. I did not see anything, Doctor."

The Doctor was in complete disbelief. This was a miracle. "We have to contact his family and contact the Special Investigating Medical Unit of the hospital immediately."

The nurse agreed to his command and contacted both the fireman's family and the special investigating unit.

The Doctor stepped near the fireman again and said, "Give him oxygen and perform an overall evaluation of his vitals, and let's see what has occurred with the condition of his wounds right away!"

The very same nurse came back within a minute with vitals. "All his vitals are stable and amazingly normal, Doctor, especially with all the traumatic burn injuries that he presented to the ER and the Burn Intensive Care Unit."

This was a miracle that even the fireman's family was shocked to process. They were still in disbelief but were joyous.

The nurse contacted the Special Investigating Medical Unit and was greeted on the phone by Dr. Carla Menita, the head scientist, who was a liaison between the hospital and the CDC. Her department looked into unique instances of disease and miraculous events like this that involved research and explanation.

Dr. Menita received the call and spoke on the line, "Hello! Dr. Menita! Special Investigative Unit. How may I help you?"

The stressed nurse spoke with great exhaustion and worry in her voice, "Hello, Dr. Menita, we have a unique situation on our hands. A Fireman was presented to our burn unit with over 60% of his body burned from an explosion and a chest puncture wound."

Dr. Manita was confused as to why she was contacted in this case. "Well, why are you calling me for a burn unit patient that was presented to the burn unit? Is this a new, unique case of a chemical burn or environmental catastrophe?"

The nurse answered her, "No, Dr. Menita, this patient presented with third-degree burns over 60% of his body…but today he is completely recovered from his burn injuries, and even his puncture wounds are healed as well. It doesn't make sense."

Dr. Menita was flabbergasted. The nurse continued speaking, "Dr. Cartwell is requesting your presence as soon as possible to explain this to the medical staff and his family. We have followed burn unit protocol and have no answers for what has occurred with this fireman patient. Dr. Cartwell does not understand this miraculous overnight healing in this case. The family and the media will soon follow up with questions. Please hurry over."

After a brief pause, Dr. Menita said, "Oh wow… that is a miracle for real! I have never heard of anything like this. I am heading there right now. I will see the Doctor within the hour. And please! The patient's immediate family can see him, but please do not let any media or any outside people around this patient until I get there with our investigating team."

The nurse obliged her command and notified Dr. Cartwell. The fireman was now calm and surrounded by his family members, his wife in his arms, shedding tears of happiness and disbelief.

"Yes, Doctor, I will inform Dr. Cartwell that you and your investigating team are coming over immediately." The nurse said that and hung up the phone.

***

As nothing goes according to plan, word got out after one of the nurses tweeted about it. Soon, this news was noticed by the local media, and it caused a group of reporters to gather outside the hospital to find out more about this instance.

As this news was trending, it hit Tamara's Twitter news feed as well, and she got super excited and rushed to share it with her friends, too. She went to the lab the following day to meet her friends.

When she spotted Courtney, she excitedly said, "Hey Courtney, check this out. I saw this on my Twitter feed this morning, and the news is all the rage on the local news reports today, too.

"What is it about?" Courtney asked, thinking it might be some celebrity gossip that Tamara would be so excited about. Little did she know that it was not the case.

Tamara once again said excitedly, "A fireman who had sustained a fire injury that consumed over 60% of his body one week ago is today completely healed! All the doctors are stunned, as they have no medical explanation for this."

She took a breath and continued, "The man was even blind, and his sight was even restored in his burned eye. I mean, his flesh has been restored to normal, like overnight! It is like a damn miracle or something, for real! Look at this girl. Wow!"

Courtney was astonished. "Oh My God! That is a miracle; I swear that medicine today is something you know. Wow, God is good; that is a real miracle!"

As Courtney and Tamara were still talking, Candace came into the lab and called out to them and said, "Hey, you guys! Come to the lounge where the fireman is on TV, and the hospital is holding a press conference about his miraculous recovery. The news media are calling this a modern-day miracle, but no one knows how or what they gave him that made him heal so rapidly."

As this news was already hyped up, and they wanted to know more about it, Courtney and Tamara followed Candace to the TV lounge to watch the press conference. The press conference was where the media shared the first glimpses of the fireman, and the fireman was also a part of the press conference. He was physically there to answer all the questions.

The new report first showed a snapshot of the fireman's initial burn injuries, and everyone in the media was simply stunned. After a while, they started the questioning session.

One of the reporters on the TV asked the fireman, "So, sir, what do you attribute your miracle of healing to today?"

The fireman smiled, and tears of happiness flew down his cheeks. Then he looked at the cameras and the reporters and prepared to respond.

"I can't tell you what I felt as the roof broke from under me and the blast of heat took me over. I felt my face and arm literally burn instantly, and I just knew I was going to die. I simply prayed and screamed, and that is all I can remember from the hit of the blast."

He paused, looked at the doctors, and continued, "God and these great doctors worked a miracle. I can't even believe my recovery today. I look at myself with astonishment because I have no pain today. It is a miracle; that is all I can say. Truly, it is. I am glad I got another chance at life today.'

The reporters wanted to ask more questions, but the hospital staff didn't allow them, and the fireman was then carried away from the TV reporters.

Candace, sitting in the lounge watching this news on TV with her friends, said, "I can't believe it; that was a real miracle! Wow... I told you guys they would have him on the news today. He is one truly lucky guy, for real."

"I think it is great that he can go home to his family again after being in a fire like that," Tamara commented.

Courtney added, "Yes, that is right; no one can take credit for that miracle for real. That was a real miracle. Wow, that made me almost cry for his great opportunity for life again."

The entire day, all three girls kept thinking and talking about this incident on various occasions, but as their college day ended, they all left the college campus building and went home.

***

In the hospital, Dr. Menita met Dr. Cartwell and his nursing team to inquire what may have happened to the patient who healed miraculously. The meeting, no doubt, was joyful but also full of questions, as everyone was stunned and had no valid reason to explain the miraculous event.

Dr. Menita, to continue her research, ordered blood samples from the fireman and asked them to be sent to a special lab for testing. She also asked the staff to run a detailed physical examination on the fireman, and all his evaluations returned normal and optimal.

As the hospital staff and Dr. Menita weren't able to understand the reason behind this miracle, another major incident took place. A patient was admitted to the hospital in a pretty serious condition.

It was an Asian family who faced a fatal car accident, and the mother was in a pretty serious condition.

She was brought to the trauma unit and was losing a lot of blood from the obvious injuries sustained in her crash. Her blood pressure was below normal due to internal bleeding noted in the OR. The doctors were trying to suture and clamp tears in her peritoneal cavity from the sustained trauma.

The doctor called for more blood to be brought to the patient, and they brought the same blood that was transfused to the fireman.

As soon as the pint reached the patient, the blood was ready to be transfused into the patient as it was hung intravenously on the medical dispensing pole. The condition of this woman was so bad that the doctors had no hope.

But once again, miraculously, as soon as the blood started transfusing in the patient's veins, her condition stabilized, and all her vitals returned to normal. The woman was kept in the ICU, and within a few hours, her wounds began to heal, her broken bones began to mend, and the lacerations in her head and face were miraculously healed.

In another medical OR, another little Asian girl, who was the daughter of the woman who was brought to the hospital after the car crash, was being treated for multiple injuries.

She had a broken femur bone, a fractured skull, facial and arm lacerations, and numerous internal injuries. Similar to her mother, she also lost a lot of blood and required a blood transfusion to sustain normal blood volume in her body from blood loss.

The girl was almost dead, as most of her vital organs were giving up on her. She had a ruptured lung, which meant she was unable to breathe. The medical teams called a medical code and tried one last time to save her.

Just like her mother, she was also transfused with the blood that Courtney donated, and as soon as blood entered her body, the little girl coughed and began to breathe normally again.

In addition to that, her lacerations began to heal right in front of the doctors and the nurses as they stood astonished. No matter what they said, they had no explanation for this. This was one of the most obvious miracles, taking place right before their eyes.

The staff in the OR, as I said, was stunned, as the girl who was almost dead was healed entirely, and that too, in front of them. The doctor slowly approached the little girl to check and saw that her leg had begun to straighten out with healing tissue, filling in the open tissue in the thigh area.

The medical team was amazed at how her blood pressure was regulated, the oxygen saturation in her blood returned to normal, and the child started breathing independently.

No one says a word. The doctor then ordered an X-ray to confirm whether the leg and the skull still had a fracture, with which the child was presented to the OR. The x-ray revealed that the femur bone was healed and normal. Similarly, the skull's fracture was also completely healed.

The doctor then called for an orthopedic to confirm the X-rays before the patient was admitted to the ICU. The orthopedic surgeon confirmed that all her fractures were healed completely. After a proper examination, the little girl was shifted to the ICU and kept under examination.

The medical investigation team was once again called and informed about this miracle. Dr. Menita was truly baffled and stunned by this new miracle at another hospital. She ordered her investigation team to go there and start an investigation to find out what led up to the miracle of the mother and the daughter both recovering from their injuries.

Dr. Menita ordered that all the news of these miracles be kept under wraps until she knew more about what may be causing these miracles to occur at these hospitals.

CHAPTER 6

Rise of the Sacred League of Death and Destruction

Meanwhile, Courtney came home and was greeted by her parents. They were already seated in front of the TV, so Courtney joined them. They were watching the news report when a reporter started narrating the fireman's miraculous recovery.

Marcus comments on the report, breaking the silence, "You know, baby, that is amazing how the fireman has been given a second chance at life. That is simply amazing."

Zephora replied, "I agree. This makes me believe in miracles again. I know that the fireman's family has to be happy over his great luck that he recovered so well."

Everyone in the room agreed. Courtney vocalized her opinion, "Yeah, Mom, I saw this news story at the college today, and I cannot believe it either. No one can explain it." She continued after a pause, as both of her parents had her attention now. "One news reporter said that he did not think his original injuries were that bad, but the doctor revealed how bad they were at the press conference. Now everyone agrees that this was truly a miracle for real."

Zephora went to the kitchen and opened the oven to pull out the chicken strips she had kept there as a snack. Marcus continued the conversation with Courtney, "Yes, Courtney, miracles still happen, you know. We only have to appreciate them when they occur. I am sure the doctors and medical personnel are going crazy trying to explain this phenomenon to each other. I would only want a court-side seat as the medical doctors try to explain this miracle."

The three of them then began to eat the chicken strips and got lost in the sentiment of this tender moment. The moment is interrupted by Cadance's call on Courtney's phone. She gleefully started speaking the moment Courtney picked up the call. "Courtney, you will never guess what just happened again. There was another miracle at another hospital. This time, there were two people, a mother and a daughter. The son just tweeted about his mother's quickly recovering health status and his sister's as well. He even showed the crash in his tweet. I don't know what is going on, but everyone is talking about this."

Courtney was left in awe. How could this be happening again? She was in shock. "Oh my God, wow! I wonder what is truly going on for real! I think that is great news, but what is causing these amazing healings to take place? I can only hope that it continues. It is amazing that people are recovering from these injuries the way they are."

***

Dr. Menita had been calling the lab at every 30-minute interval to get some sort of answer. She was curious as to what was enabling this fast recovery. There must have been some sign in the blood that would have answers. Her queries were answered when the lab had the reports ready.

"The blood samples are normal. However, there is a unique high-protein molecule that all the patients have in common with each other. This special protein marker is like an energy booster or extra engine in the blood cells that may explain why the blood cells can repair tissue at such a fast rate."

Dr. Menita was gagged at this discovery and decided to hold a press conference. She and all the doctors and medical teams tried to explain this phenomenon. "We have to find out what has caused this very unique phenomenon in our hospitals. Before this word gets out to the public, we need answers. I am trying to limit the fact that various health organizations are constantly calling us up to see if we are using any new medical agents on our citizens. We know this is not the case. We then have to come up with logical scientific solutions to what is causing these so-called miracles to take place. Does anyone know how these circumstances could have taken place in the hospitals this week?"

Silence took over the room, as nobody had any clue. Slowly, people started whispering and discussing with one another. Everyone was in a state of bewilderment and yet had no answer. Suddenly, a voice boomed from the back of the room, and everyone looked around. It was Bryan Domenico, a US government representative.

He introduced himself and explained how the US government would take over this operation's investigative machinery. "I am here on behalf of the US government to find out what is going on with these miracles. This is now a government investigation, and we will find out what medical intervention may be of use in the hospital networks here."

As this was no answer to her question, Dr. Menita got pissed. He continued to give her commands, "I want to be informed of every medication and code protocol used in each patient. You will keep me informed of every detail. We must find out what has healed these people so that our government and policies will be protected from those who would use this miraculous healing against the US."

Dr. Menita was pissed at the audacity. "Wow, I never thought that the US government would come here and find out how our hospitals help people heal. It usually goes the other way around." She continued speaking in a condescending tone. "It seems like you all are often here to cut funding and make miracles impossible to happen for average Americans just trying to stay alive."

Bryan ignored her sarcasm as a euphemism and said, "Dr. Menita, I represent the US government and its interests. It seems that you have a unique occurrence, or a miracle, as the press is calling it. Would you think it would be wise if this miracle were used in the wrong hands? Imagine how it could cause a city to panic or, worse, destabilize our entire way of life. Miracles are great, but if you don't know how they occurred, it could be a tool to put us all in the wrong hands. I will not be satisfied until I know what is causing this miracle to happen, and you will bring me this satisfaction."

Dr. Menita understood the gravity of the situation, but she still needed to ensure she had control over it. "You will have access to all our information and processes from the data we gather. What I ask is that your people do not get in the way of hospital protocol or routine operations and do not report any findings in the press or media. All discoveries will be reported to me, evaluated by my medical science team first, and passed on to you without interference. I am sure we will have enough to deal with our hospitals turning into religious shrines by the media." She then addressed everyone in the room, "This meeting is adjourned. Thank you all."

***

Dr. Menita continued with her search for answers. She contacted her medical college colleague, Dr. Kathy Greensberg. She was a specialist in medical history and religious science phenomena. She worked in the city and was often consulted on special cases that bordered on medical, scientific, and religious origins.

She was connected to Dr. Greensberg's secretary and requested to speak to Dr. Greensberg. The secretary asked for her credentials and the purpose of the call. Dr. Menita channeled the sense of urgency and said, "My name is Dr. Menita. Please tell Dr. Greensberg that this is important. Thank you." Not a minute later, the two were connected.

"Hi, this is Dr. Greensberg. How may I help you?"

Dr. Menita sighed and said, "Hey Kathy, it's me, Carla. I have a real situation going on at the local hospitals here in the city, and I know I will need your help to narrow down what's going on."

Kathy was taken aback to hear Carla's voice and said, "Oh, I hope all is well. Are you doing okay, Carla?"

Dr. Menita was confused as to where she would start speaking. "Well, I am doing okay, but we have had a few miracles that are unexplainable over the last two weeks. People have started to heal almost overnight, and one case was simply instantly."

Kathy was unimpressed and replied, "I thought in your line of work, that would be a great thing. What is so bad about these cases?"

'Here comes the hard part,' Dr. Menita thought. "Yeah, you got a point there, but when you have three cases of broken bones healing instantly, lung puncture wounds closing and healing in one hour, and burn wounds healing in less than an hour, you can imagine everyone is getting somewhat concerned and alarmed because the hospitals do not know what the miracle's cause is."

Kathy was impressed now. "Oh wow, are you serious, Carla? I am truly interested. It sounds like you have a real situation on your hands. But since you are calling me, you must feel that it is a miracle that is more than medical research can explain."

Dr. Menita replied, "Yes, this is something that I will need. I will need you and your team to help me solve this situation. I know I cannot solve this situation with medical research alone, so please help me out. Also, please remember, we cannot take any of this to the media."

Dr. Greensberg understood the situation. "I do understand the discretion, and my team will start right away. I have been following the miraculous events on the news, but I am sure you will have more important facts that the media will not have to report. What do you think is causing this unique finding in nature?"

Dr. Menita replied, "I have to admit, Kathy, at this point, I am simply baffled. The medical teams and doctors are taking the appropriate steps to treat each patient, providing standard antibiotic therapy, blood transfusions, sustained fluid volume, and maintaining oxygen levels in lung tissue. Everything has been looked at. So far, all the blood samples from each patient have been sent to the laboratory for analysis."

Kathy was completely on board now, and Carla had her complete support. "Alright, I will need to interview all the patients with my team and evaluate their medical history while making their physical and mental charts. I will also need access to the religious, cognitive, and mental ability charts. This may involve a supernatural ability that may affect each patient."

Dr. Menita was ready to give anything and everything to her. "I can and will give you whatever you need. Just make sure that you report any of your findings directly to me and not the government representative, Bryan Domenico. I feel he could be dangerous and compromise these events' findings."

"Sure thing, Carla, I will only report to you. I will be contacting a special investigating unit of clergy that looks into events like this. My organization has scientists and historians that could be very helpful in finding the answers you need."

Dr. Menita took a sigh of relief. She was happy to have built a small yet trustable support system around her. "Sounds great, Kathy. I am open to your investigative approach. Just keep everything between us. Remember that our findings are not to be shared with anyone."

CHAPTER 7

Revelation of a Divine Prophesy over the Science of Evil

Zachary was a fresh college graduate who was now working in the laboratory as an assistant. He was Courtney's senior in college; the two dated briefly in college but hadn't met in a long time. However, they still had some lingering feelings for one another.

Zachary was studying the blood samples and noticed a special energy protein marker in the patient's blood that was collected after their miracles. The protein marker was not there prior to the blood transfusion. He quickly called his supervisor to report his findings.

He explained to his supervisor in a serious tone, "Hey, there are some unique properties found in these blood samples from these patients so far. It seems that there is some organelle made up of protein. A special nuclei energy cell gives their blood a special property to reproduce itself or even repair tissues. This is done by carrying more oxygen to tissue so that RBC can accelerate with this protein around."

The supervisor was astounded. He was surprised at this finding. "Are you sure of what you have found, Zachery? This isn't something that should be left to guesswork, son. Make sure you double-check any findings and verify every marker that seems significant."

Zachary agreed with the supervisor's concern, but he had already done his research thoroughly. "Sir, I've already done so. I

After a short pause, she continued, "This is the type of case that I need your expertise in. I need an explanation for how a miracle like this can happen."

Dr. Phillip was quick to share his opinion, "You know God has never stopped existing; it is simply mankind that tries to rule out true miracles and genuine acts of greatness in nature. We simply try to give God his due credit with our methods to point out that mankind is not as powerful as a natural occurrence of what only God can take credit for."

Dr. Greensberg understood and knew this but needed strong evidence to prove it to Dr. Menita and others. "I know what you do, doctor. What I need is a true evaluation of these miracles from your point of view, and I only want your findings to be reported to me."

She then explained to him why such secrecy was desirable, "The US Government is now involved, and many other corporations and pharmaceutical companies may be following this case of miracles that has actually healed human tissues with an almost instant recovery. There is no modern medical application that can take credit for these occurrences, Dr. Michael. This is exactly why we need your evaluation of these cases."

He replied to Dr. Greensberg, "I acknowledge the recent surge in miraculous events that have challenged our understanding of faith and the divine. I'm ready to begin immediately. Access to all patient data and the investigative methods used by the medical team will be crucial for my analysis. In the event that I identify a key factor or individual responsible for these miracles, how do you propose we proceed with this discovery?"

Dr. Greensberg replied, "If our miracle just happens to be a person, then you can imagine the intrigue that would encircle such a person with this type of human ability. I am not sure what may happen to the being, but I'm sure modern scientists will try to examine and learn from them."

After a brief pause, once Dr. Phillips had processed this information, he said, "It would be a living hell for a person that had the ability to heal other people. There would instantly be a conflict between the Church and governments worldwide. Remember what happened to Jesus and all the disciples? Anyone who could connect and heal society has been assassinated or imprisoned, even if they used their power for good. It is human nature to be most afraid of what is not understood or challenge a set form of authority."

"Historical precedents have repeatedly demonstrated the dangers faced by those who possess extraordinary abilities."

This was something Dr. Greensberg was well aware of.

"Yes, Dr. Phillips, this is precisely why our primary goal must be to ascertain whether these miracles result from an extraordinary individual. We must prevent the potential exploitation or mistreatment of such a person, who might otherwise be treated inhumanely or exploited for their unique abilities," she said in response.

Dr. Phillips concurred, "I understand the gravity of our task. We'll commence the investigation into these miraculous events immediately and keep you fully informed. This investigation might lead us to an unprecedented understanding of divine intervention in human affairs."

Dr. Greensberg, feeling confident in her approach, shook Dr. Phillips' hand in agreement before departing. After she left, Dr. Phillips, with a look of deep contemplation and concern, made a phone call, murmuring, "This could be a groundbreaking discovery."

Hours later, Dr. Phillips and Dr. Greensberg met with the fireman who had miraculously recovered from his injuries and was now resting with his family.

Dr. Phillips began, "Thank you for allowing us this time with you. Your recovery is truly remarkable."

The fireman, equally astounded, replied, "I'm just as surprised. I never expected to survive that fire."

Dr. Greensberg then inquired, "Can you recall any sensations or visions during your unconsciousness, either in the ambulance or the hospital?"

The fireman recounted his experience, "I remember the intense pain from the explosion, then blacking out. On the way to the hospital, the pain was unbearable. I was bleeding heavily. But then, a warm sensation spread through my body, and the pain started fading. It was miraculous. My vision, which was lost, returned. I believe the medical staff gave me a transfusion and something through my IV, and then I lost consciousness again."

Dr. Greensberg asked further, "Did you feel at any point like you were dying?"

He responded, visibly emotional, "The thought of dying, especially not seeing my daughter again, was terrifying. But the warmth that enveloped me gave me hope, and my pain subsided almost instantly. It felt like I was going to make it."

Dr. Phillips understood his emotions and said, "Thank you for sharing your incredible story. Should you recall any more details, don't hesitate to get in touch with me." Handing his card, he added, "One more question – do you believe divine intervention played a role in your recovery?"

After a moment of reflection, the fireman replied, "Given my injuries, I should either be dead or facing a long, painful recovery. But here I am with my family, unscathed and able to see again. I can only attribute this to a miracle, a divine act beyond human comprehension."

Dr. Phillips concluded the interview, "Thank you for sharing your story with us." The two doctors then left the fireman's home, deeply pondering the implications of their conversation. In their car, they discussed the undeniable presence of a divine element in these events. "We're witnessing a real miracle, something beyond the scope of current medical understanding," Dr. Phillips remarked.

Dr. Greensberg agreed, "Absolutely. It's crucial that we explore similar historical cases of miraculous healings. The way he recovered is nothing short of extraordinary."

Meanwhile, Dr. Menita received a long-awaited call from the lab supervisor. Eagerly answering, she said, "This is Dr. Menita. How can I assist?"

The voice on the other end conveyed groundbreaking news. "Dr. Menita, we've discovered a unique protein marker in all the patients' blood post-transfusion. This marker wasn't present before."

Startled, Dr. Menita fumbled with her coffee, quickly reaching for a pen. "Are these findings confirmed? We can't afford any inaccuracies."

The supervisor assured her, "Absolutely. We've triple-checked the data. This marker is unprecedented in normal red blood cells."

Dr. Menita, overwhelmed by the implications, instructed, "Send me the detailed blood analysis and ensure all samples are securely stored. This information is classified. Also, dispatch a sample to the CDC immediately."

"Understood, Dr. Menita. I'm on it," the supervisor replied.

Exhausted, Dr. Menita sat down, studying the incoming fax of the blood report. Overwhelmed by the enormity of the discovery, she reclined, staring at the ceiling, too tired to move, eventually falling asleep in her chair.

In a parallel development, a gang member, severely wounded and losing blood, was rushed to the hospital. Initially, the blood he received wasn't from Courtney. Shortly after, his condition worsened; his blood pressure plummeted, and he began to convulse.

In the ER, a blood transfusion was urgently administered. While tending to the young man's injuries, the attending physician witnessed an inexplicable phenomenon: the tissues began to repair themselves. "Record this," he instructed the nurse. "It's like witnessing an invisible force at work."

The patient's condition stabilized as they watched, and the wounds started healing rapidly. The astounded medical team stepped back, observing the miraculous recovery. The surgeon, in disbelief, tested the healing by making a small incision, which healed instantly.

After ensuring the patient's vitals were normal, the doctor ordered blood samples for further analysis. The entire event was captured on camera, leaving the medical staff in a state of shock and wonder. The patient, now stable, was moved to the recovery room, with the medical team hesitant to disturb the miraculous scene. The hospital corridor buzzed with awe-struck doctors, nurses, and staff, all struggling to comprehend the extraordinary healing they had just witnessed.

***

Meanwhile, Courtney and Tamara were casually chatting in Courtney's living room, with the news playing in the background on TV. Their conversation paused abruptly when a news report featuring a laboratory caught their attention. Zachary, someone familiar to them, appeared on the screen.

"Look, it's Zachery on TV!" Courtney exclaimed in surprise. "I had no idea he was working in that lab. I've got to call him!"

Tamara teased her, noticing Courtney's interest. "You two were close last year, weren't you? He'd be glad to hear from you."

Courtney, trying to play it cool, responded, "Well, it's been a while, but yeah, I'll give him a call."

Tamara, smiling knowingly, stood up to leave. "I'll let you catch up with him then. Keep me updated, okay? Love you!"

After Tamara left, Courtney dialed Zachary's number. He answered, clearly pleased to hear from her. Their conversation quickly turned to the news segment.

Zachary explained, "We're researching a miraculous event you've probably heard about. But keep it under wraps, okay? It's confidential."

Courtney, amused, promised to keep his secret. "Don't worry, your 'Clark Kent' identity is safe with me."

Their conversation turned lighter, reminiscing about their time together at the university lab and sharing a laugh over a past mishap.

"I'd like to see you again," Courtney said, a hint of affection in her voice.

Zachary responded warmly, "I'd like that too. My schedule is hectic, but I can make time this weekend if you're free."

"Sounds perfect. Let's plan for this weekend," she replied.

They ended the call with plans to meet, leaving Courtney smiling to herself, excited about the reunion.

CHAPTER 8

Echoes of a Dark Pursuit

The sterile, crisp air of the hospital corridor did little to calm Dr. Menita's racing heart as she hurried toward the ICU. Her phone call earlier that morning had been abrupt but unmistakable – another miraculous healing had occurred. Her mind was a whirlwind of thoughts and possibilities as she navigated the maze of white hallways.

Reaching the ICU, she was greeted by the hushed but urgent atmosphere typical of the place. Nurses moved with efficient grace, their faces etched with a blend of concern and awe. Dr. Menita's strides were quick, her lab coat billowing slightly with her pace.

"Dr. Franklin!" she called out, spotting the trauma physician near a patient's room. Her voice cut through the muted beeps and soft whispers, turning a few heads.

Dr. Franklin, a woman of about forty with an air of composed professionalism, turned to face Dr. Menita. Her expression was a complex reflection of astonishment and solemnity.

"Dr. Menita, I've never seen anything like this," Dr. Franklin began, her voice barely above a whisper as if afraid to disturb the miraculous tranquility that seemed to envelop the room. "The patient... he literally healed right there on the OR table. An incision in his abdomen just... closed on its own."

Dr. Menita's brows furrowed, her scientific mind grappling with the implications of what she was hearing. "Are you certain? This goes beyond any medical explanation. What about the nurses? Did anyone talk to the media?"

Dr. Franklin shook her head. "Our entire team witnessed it. We even recorded the event, Dr. Menita. But as for the media, I can't be sure who might have leaked this news. You know how quickly word spreads."

"We need to control this narrative," Dr. Menita said firmly, her gaze sharp and focused. "The last thing we need is a citywide panic or… or a religious outbreak of fanatics breaking down these walls, looking for some miracle cure. Have you informed the family yet?"

"Not yet," Dr. Franklin replied, her eyes reflecting a mix of apprehension and duty. "We were waiting for you. The CDC hasn't given us any directive on how to proceed with these inexplicable healings."

"Tell the family he's stable, recovering from anesthesia in the ICU. We need time to draw blood and perform evaluations before they see him. By then, we might have a better idea of how to explain this… this new miracle."

Dr. Franklin nodded, her face set in a mask of professional resolve. "Understood, Dr. Menita. What about the other cases? The fireman, the Asian family…"

Dr. Menita exhaled a slow release of pent-up tension. "We're looking into it. This is the fourth event in two days, Dr. Franklin. Something unprecedented is happening in our city."

As Dr. Menita stepped into the patient's room, she saw the young man lying peacefully, his wounds inexplicably healed. The room was silent except for the steady beeping of the heart monitor. She approached the bed, her mind racing with questions that science alone couldn't answer.

Outside, the world remained oblivious to the extraordinary events unfolding within these walls. But inside, in the quiet of the ICU, Dr. Menita stood on the precipice of a discovery that could change the course of medical history. The truth lay there, in the veins of the miraculously healed, a secret waiting to be unraveled.

***

The sun shone through the blinds of Dr. Kathy Greensberg's office as she sat, phone pressed to her ear, her eyes scanning the array of patient data before her. Beside her, Dr. Jon Michael Phillips leaned forward, his gaze intense, as he listened to the conversation on speakerphone.

"Yes, Kathy, we have another one at St. Emanuel Hospital," Dr. Menita's voice crackled over the line, edged with a mix of excitement and anxiety. "There's video evidence and multiple staff witnesses."

Dr. Greensberg's fingers drummed lightly on her desk. "We just left the fireman's residence," she began, her voice measured. "He described a warm sensation coursing through his body, beginning at his arms, shortly after the blood transfusion. Then he blacked out."

Phillips interjected, his voice a deep timbre, "And we've found a unique marker in the blood samples from three patients so far. If it matches with this latest case, we might be dealing with a very special donor."

Kathy's eyes narrowed thoughtfully. "A donor…" she mused, tapping her chin. "This is potentially groundbreaking, but we must tread carefully. The implications are enormous."

Phillips nodded, his face a mask of concentration. "We need to understand the full extent of these phenomena. Could it be a genetic anomaly, or something more?"

The phone call ended with a mutual agreement to reconvene once more data was gathered. Dr. Greensberg turned to Phillips, her expression serious. "Let's visit the recovery room. We need to see this for ourselves."

In the recovery room, they found the patient resting, the very picture of health where once grave injuries had been. Nurses moved around, their expressions a mixture of disbelief and reverence.

Approaching the bed, Greensberg observed the patient closely. "Remarkable," she whispered, her eyes wide, "to think this is the result of a blood transfusion."

Phillips leaned closer, his brow furrowed. "It defies all our medical understanding. The speed of recovery, the completeness of it… it's unlike anything I've ever seen."

Greensberg nodded slowly. "We need to explore every possibility. Genetic factors, environmental influences... and, of course, the blood donor."

Phillips glanced around the room, then back at Greensberg. "If it's true, if there really is someone out there with this... ability, the consequences could be unprecedented."

Greensberg's eyes met Phillips'. "We're on the verge of something monumental, Jon. This could redefine everything we know about medicine, about the very essence of healing."

Phillips sighed, a mix of excitement and trepidation in his eyes. "And yet, we must be cautious. If word gets out about a 'miracle' blood donor, it could lead to chaos, exploitation..."

Greensberg placed a hand on his shoulder, her gaze steady. "Which is why we must find the truth, Jon. For the sake of those healed, for the donor, and for the future of medical science."

As they left the recovery room, the weight of their discovery hung heavily between them. Outside the hospital walls, life went on as usual. But within, in the quiet corridors and sterile rooms, a mystery was unfolding – a mystery that promised to change the world in ways they could scarcely imagine.

***

Meanwhile, in the quiet, well-tended living room of the Ayako residence, a sense of serene normalcy prevailed, a stark contrast to the miraculous event that had recently touched this family. Dr. Kathy Greensberg and Dr. Jon Michael Phillips sat across from Mrs. Ayako, who held a rosary in her hands, her expression a blend of gratitude and wonder.

"Mrs. Ayako, thank you for allowing us to speak with you today," Dr. Greensberg began, her voice gentle yet filled with curiosity. "We're investigating the remarkable recovery you and your daughter experienced. Could you describe what happened?"

Mrs. Ayako, a delicate woman in her mid-thirties, nodded slowly, her eyes reflecting the enormity of her experience. "I still find it hard to believe," she started, her voice soft but clear. "After the accident, I was trapped in the car, in so much pain… I thought I was going to die."

Dr. Phillips leaned forward attentively. "What happened next, Mrs. Ayako? Did you feel anything unusual?"

Her fingers tightened around the rosary. "Yes, in the hospital. There was this warm sensation… like a wave of calmness washing over me. My leg, which was broken, started feeling… different. The pain receded, and it felt like someone was realigning it from the inside."

Dr. Greensberg exchanged a glance with Dr. Phillips, her mind racing. "And you were given a blood transfusion during this time?"

Mrs. Ayako nodded. "Yes, I lost a lot of blood. The nurses kept saying so. But after the transfusion, everything changed. It was like a miracle."

Phillips interjected, "And your daughter? She experienced something similar?"

Mrs. Ayako's eyes filled with tears. "She was declared dead on the operating table. But then, miraculously, she came back. She told me later that she felt a warm, comforting presence, like an angel was with her."

The room fell silent, the weight of her words hanging in the air. Dr. Greensberg finally spoke, her voice gentle. "Mrs. Ayako, do you believe what happened to you and your daughter was a miracle?"

With a firm nod, Mrs. Ayako replied, "Absolutely. There's no other explanation. My faith tells me it was God's work."

Dr. Phillips, ever the scientist, pondered aloud, "And yet, the timing with the blood transfusion… it's too coincidental. There must be a scientific explanation."

Dr. Greensberg stood up, her mind abuzz with thoughts. "Mrs. Ayako, your story is incredible. It gives us much to think about. Thank you for sharing it with us."

For Dr. Greensberg and Dr. Phillips, the mystery deepened, a puzzle that was scientific and perhaps something more.

***

Later, within the grand conference room of the hospital, under the bright clinical lights, a group of esteemed medical professionals, government agents, and scientists gathered around a large oval table. The air was charged with anticipation and a hint of nervous energy. Dr. Menita stood at the head of the table, clearing her throat to address the room.

"Thank you all for coming on such short notice," Dr. Menita began, her voice resonating with authority. "We're here to discuss a groundbreaking discovery in our recent cases of miraculous recoveries."

Dr. Greensberg, seated near the front, leaned forward. "Dr. Menita, are you referring to the unique protein and nuclei found in the blood of the recovered patients?"

Dr. Menita nodded, her eyes scanning the room. "Precisely, Dr. Greensberg. Our lab has confirmed that a special protein, coupled with a unique type of nuclei, is present in all the miraculously healed patients. And this was not in their blood prior to receiving transfusions."

Sitting beside Dr. Greensberg, Dr. Phillips interjected, "And you believe this is due to a blood donor?"

Dr. Menita affirmed, "Yes, our evidence strongly suggests that these healing properties are coming from a specific blood donor. Furthermore, this donor is likely female, based on the presence of coagulation factor FV and Alpha-1-antitrypsin markers."

The room erupted in murmurs of disbelief and fascination. Bryan Domenico, the government pharmaceutical agent present at the meeting, spoke up, his voice tinged with excitement. "This is incredible! Do you realize the potential implications? We could be on the verge of medical breakthroughs previously unimaginable!"

Dr. Menita raised a hand to calm the room. "While the potential is vast, we must approach this with utmost caution and respect for the donor's privacy and rights."

Dr. Phillips nodded in agreement. "This isn't just a scientific discovery; it's a human one. We must remember that at the heart of this is an individual whose life could be turned upside down by this revelation."

The discussion continued, with different voices chiming in with questions and speculations. Dr. Greensberg, however, seemed lost in thought, her gaze distant. "If we find this donor, what then? How do we proceed, ethically and medically?"

Dr. Menita looked around the room, her expression solemn. "Our priority is to find and protect this individual. We need to understand the full extent and limitations of these properties. But let me be clear – no action will be taken without full consent."

Bryan Domenico leaned back in his chair, his mind racing with possibilities. "The government's interest is in the public health potential. Imagine the lives that could be saved, the ailments that could be cured!"

Dr. Phillips countered, "And yet, we must not lose sight of the individual at the center of this. We cannot allow this discovery to be exploited."

As the meeting drew to a close, Dr. Menita's final words resonated in the room. "This is a new frontier in medicine, one that requires our best ethical judgment and scientific expertise. Let's proceed with caution, respect, and an unshakable commitment to doing what's right."

The room emptied slowly, the attendees lost in their own thoughts, grappling with the enormity of the discovery and the weight of responsibility that came with it. In the world of medicine, a new chapter was being written, one that blurred the lines between science and miracles.

***

After the meeting concluded, Bryan Domenico sat in a secluded corner of a bar, nursing a drink. Across from him, Detective Jeffrey Thompson, with his rugged demeanor and an air of nonchalance, leaned back in his chair.

Domenico's voice was low but carried a sense of urgency. "Detective Thompson, I trust you understand the gravity of what I'm about to ask you?"

Thompson, his eyes scanning the room, nodded slightly. "I have a good idea, Domenico. But why don't you spell it out for me, just to be clear?"

Domenico leaned forward, his eyes locking onto Thompson's. "We need to find a particular individual. A blood donor. This isn't your typical search – this person, this woman, holds the key to a medical revolution."

Thompson's eyebrows rose slightly, a smirk playing at the corner of his mouth. "Sounds like you're hunting for a needle in a haystack. What makes her so special?"

Domenico's voice dropped to a whisper, tinged with a mix of excitement and caution. "Her blood… it has properties. Healing properties like we've never seen. We're talking about the potential to revolutionize medicine."

Thompson whistled softly, leaning in. "And you want me to find her. What's in it for me?"

Domenico's lips curled into a half-smile. "Let's just say the reward will be substantial. You'll be compensated handsomely for your discretion and efficiency."

Thompson's eyes narrowed thoughtfully. "All right, I'm in. But I work my way – off the books. And I want half the payment upfront."

Domenico nodded, a plan already forming in his mind. "Agreed. But understand this, Thompson – we need her unharmed. She's no use to us if she's… damaged."

Thompson leaned back, his expression hardening. "You'll get your miracle worker, Domenico. Just make sure my account reflects your gratitude."

As the two men rose to leave, Domenico paused, his voice laced with a final warning. "Remember, Thompson, this stays between us. If this leaks, it'll be more than just your reputation on the line."

Thompson gave a grim nod, his mind already racing with the logistics of the hunt. As they exited the bar, the night air seemed to hum with the potential of what lay ahead – a game of shadows and secrets, with stakes higher than either man dared to admit.

***

In the park, under the dappled sunlight filtering through the trees, Courtney and Zachary sat on a bench near the serene lake.

"So, Zachary, this whole thing with the miracles... it's all over the news," Courtney began, her tone a mix of curiosity and disbelief. "And you're right in the middle of it all. What's it like in the lab?"

Zachary, looking out over the water, sighed deeply. "It's been surreal, Courtney. Ever since we discovered this unique protein in the blood of the healed patients, everything's been a whirlwind."

Courtney leaned in, her eyes wide. "Do you really think it's because of one person? Like, is someone's blood causing these miracles?"

Zachary nodded, a serious look on his face. "It sounds like something out of a sci-fi movie, but yes. It's looking more and more like these recoveries are linked to a blood donor."

A pause followed as Courtney processed this information. "That's... incredible. But also kind of scary, right? What if this person doesn't know about their ability?"

Zachary turned to face her, his expression grave. "That's the thing. We're not even sure they're aware. And if they are, what does that mean for them? This could change their life forever."

Courtney frowned, her mind racing with the implications. "It almost feels like a heavy burden to carry. I mean, imagine the pressure, the responsibility..."

Zachary looked at her, his eyes reflecting a mix of concern and admiration. "Exactly. And there's something else, Courtney. There's talk about finding this person. The lab, the government... everyone's interested. And I'm not sure it's all for the right reasons."

Courtney's gaze fell to her hands, clasped in her lap. "Zachary, that's frightening. This person, whoever they are, they're just a regular person, right? They could be anyone."

Zachary reached out, gently placing a hand over hers. "I know. And that's why we have to be careful about how we handle this. We're talking about someone's life here."

Courtney looked up, her eyes meeting his. "Do you think... I mean, could it be someone we know?"

Zachary's face softened, a hint of a smile appearing. "I doubt it. But in times like these, Courtney, I believe anything's possible."

***

In the hushed confines of the hospital's archive library, Dr. Greensberg and Dr. Phillips sat before an old computer, its screen illuminating pages of archived records and forgotten cases. They were on a mission to unravel the history of the recent miraculous healings.

"Look at this, Jon," Dr. Greensberg said, pointing to a faded document on the screen. "A case from fifty years ago, right here in the city. Miraculous healings, similar to what we're seeing now."

Dr. Phillips leaned in, his eyes scanning the text. "Incredible. It says here that three patients experienced instantaneous recovery after receiving blood transfusions. But there's no explanation, just like our current cases."

Greensberg's fingers danced over the keyboard, pulling up more files. "And here's another one. A month later, more unexplained recoveries. But then… nothing. It all just stopped."

Phillips rubbed his chin thoughtfully. "It's as if the phenomenon just vanished, only to resurface now. But why the gap? And what happened to these patients after they recovered?"

Greensberg clicked through another file, her brow furrowing. "This document mentions a fire at the hospital where these events occurred. It says most records were lost."

Phillips sat back, a look of frustration crossing his face. "So, we have a pattern but no leads. This is like looking for a needle in a historical haystack."

Suddenly, Greensberg's eyes lit up. "Wait, Jon. This might be something. There's a mention here of Dr. Lewis Adequa, the lead doctor on those cases. He was part of some African health alliance group."

Phillips leaned forward again, intrigued. "An African health alliance? That's an unusual detail. Do you think there's a connection between that group and the miracles?"

Greensberg's voice was thoughtful. "It's possible. The group apparently had ties with the Catholic Church. Maybe they knew something about these miraculous healings."

Phillips nodded slowly. "We should investigate this further. The Catholic Church might have records or information about this group and Dr. Adequa."

Greensberg closed the laptop, determination in her eyes. "Let's do it. We need to understand the past to solve the present mystery. I'll contact the Catholic Diocese. Maybe they can shed some light on this Dr. Adequa and the African Health Alliance."

***

The scene unfolded in the shadowy confines of an abandoned warehouse. Detective Jeffrey Thompson, his face a mask of grim determination, paced the dusty floor. His captive, a young girl, lay bound and gagged on a makeshift bed in the corner, her eyes wide with fear.

Thompson, checking his watch impatiently, muttered to himself. "This has to be the girl. She fits the description. Once I confirm her blood is the key, Domenico will pay through the nose."

The girl's muffled cries echoed in the empty space, her eyes pleading for mercy. Thompson approached her with a syringe in his hand, his expression cold and calculating.

"Don't worry, sweetheart. This won't hurt a bit. Just need a little blood for testing," he said, his voice falsely soothing as he drew a sample.

Once done, he secured the vial and sent it to Bryan Domenico for analysis. Settling down to wait, he glanced at the girl, a sense of satisfaction washing over him. He was certain he had the golden ticket in his hands.

Hours passed, and the girl sobbed quietly, her hope of rescue dwindling with each passing minute. Thompson, growing impatient, checked his phone repeatedly for any update from Domenico.

Finally, his phone buzzed. Thompson snatched it up, reading the message with growing disbelief and frustration. "Not the right match? Damn it!

Detective Thompson, realizing the enormity of his error, stood over the captive girl, his mind racing with panic. The gravity of his mistake bore down on him, and a chilling decision took root in his mind. He needed to ensure his actions remained undiscovered.

His eyes flickered with a cold, calculating glint as he stared at the message on his phone. A realization dawned on him that twisted his insides—a terrible mistake. The girl, bound and gagged in the corner, was not the miracle donor he had been desperately seeking.

As he loomed over her, a vile and corrupt impulse surged within him. The air in the warehouse grew thicker, charged with an evident sense of dread and malice. Thompson, his moral compass long shattered, saw the girl not as a victim of his grave error but as an object of his dark, twisted desires.

With a sinister intent, Thompson approached the girl. His actions, driven by a depraved greed and a complete departure from his sworn duty to protect, were of a man who had fully succumbed to his most base and vile instincts. He callously stripped her of her clothes, violating her in a manner that defied humanity.

The girl's muffled pleas and struggles were to no avail against the strength of the rogue detective. Thompson's heart had hardened to any semblance of empathy or decency. His actions were not just a betrayal of his badge but of the very essence of humanity.

After his horrendous act, Thompson, wanting to erase any evidence of his presence, beat her to the bone and administered a sedative to the girl. Her struggles ceased, leaving her in a state of vulnerable unconsciousness. He callously covered her, a mere afterthought to his vile deeds.

As he stood in the warehouse, his silhouette was that of a man who had traversed beyond redemption. His actions were not just a violation of the law but a desecration of human dignity. He had become a harbinger of evil, a stark embodiment of cruelty and corruption.

The warehouse, once just a forgotten structure, had become a scene of unspeakable horror—proof of how far one man could fall from the grace of humanity. Detective Thompson, once a guardian of the law, had devolved into a monstrous figure driven by greed and a complete disregard for human life and dignity.

His footsteps echoed hollowly as he left the warehouse, leaving behind a chilling reminder of the darkness that can reside in the human soul. The shadows seemed to whisper of his crimes, marking him as a man who had willingly embraced his descent into malevolence. Thompson's quest to find the real miracle blood donor continued, but now it was tainted with the blood of his unforgivable sins.

***

"Hey, Daddy, what are you up to today? I thought you were taking a break," Courtney said, her voice light and teasing.

Marcus Malveaux smiled at his daughter. "Well, I was planning to, but you know how it is. Always something that needs doing."

Their conversation was interrupted by the TV in the living room, where a news report was starting. A reporter's voice carried into the kitchen. "Breaking news: a young girl has gone missing in the city. Here is her photo. If you have any information, please contact the police immediately."

Courtney paused, her hand on her lunch bag, as the seriousness of the news sunk in. "Oh my God, Daddy, that's so scary. Why are people like this?"

Marcus's face hardened with concern. "Courtney, listen to me. You need to be careful. Stay with your friends, don't go anywhere alone, okay?"

Courtney nodded, though a flicker of irritation crossed her face. "Daddy, I'm always careful. I have my pepper spray, and I stay in groups. I'll be fine."

Marcus looked at her intently. "Promise me, Courtney. You're everything to me. I can't lose you."

Courtney walked over and hugged him. "I promise, Daddy. I'll be careful." Marcus's eyes still lingered on the TV screen, where the image of the missing girl was still displayed.

"Where are you off to this morning?" "I'm going to the blood drive with Tamara and Candace. Oh, and Zachary told me they've found some special protein in the blood of those miracle patients. Isn't that crazy?"

Marcus's expression softened. "It is. And speaking of Zachary, how are things with you two?"

Courtney blushed slightly. "He's special, Daddy. But we're just seeing how things go."

Marcus nodded, a protective look in his eyes. "Just remember what's important, Courtney. Your safety, your future. You're a smart girl."

"I know, Daddy. I'll see you later, okay?" Courtney gave him a quick peck on the cheek and headed out, her spirits high and oblivious to the significance of her own blood that was about to change the course of many lives.

As the door closed behind her, Marcus stood alone in the kitchen, his eyes still on the TV screen, a father's worry etched deep in his heart.

***

In the austere office of Father Samuel at the Catholic Diocese, Dr. Greensberg and Dr. Phillips sat opposite the elderly Priest. A sense of history pervaded the room, filled with old books and religious artifacts.

"Father Samuel, thank you for meeting us," Dr. Greensberg began, her voice echoing slightly in the high-ceilinged room. "We're investigating a series of miraculous healings and believe they may be connected to similar events from the past."

Father Samuel, his hands clasped over a well-worn Bible, nodded sagely. "Ah, you speak of the miracles from fifty years ago. A fascinating yet troubling time."

Dr. Phillips leaned forward, intrigued. "Troubling? In what way, Father?"

The Priest sighed, a distant look in his eyes. "The miracles were a symbol of hope, but they also brought strife. There was Dr. Lewis Adequa, a physician and a man of deep faith, who was at the center of these events."

Dr. Greensberg interjected, "Was Dr. Adequa responsible for these healings?"

Father Samuel shook his head. "No, he was merely a witness. The healings were attributed to a certain blood transfusion, much like your current cases. But the source was never identified."

Dr. Phillips' brow furrowed. "Was there any speculation about the blood donor?"

The old Priest glanced at a faded photograph on his desk, a picture of a younger him with a man of African descent. "There were whispers, Dr. Phillips. Whispers of a man with a lineage thought lost to time – a descendant of Simon of Cyrene, known for carrying the cross."

Dr. Greensberg leaned back, her mind racing. "Could it be possible that this lineage has resurfaced?"

Father Samuel's eyes twinkled. "The Lord works in mysterious ways, Dr. Greensberg. However, the miracles ceased abruptly after a tragic fire destroyed the hospital and all records."

Dr. Phillips sat up, urgency in his voice. "Father, do you know anything about the current whereabouts of this lineage?"

The Priest hesitated before replying. "There's one who might know – Bishop Abaracus of the Zebulon Priesthood. He is a guardian of ancient secrets and might have answers."

Dr. Greensberg stood up, determined in her stance. "We need to find him, Father. These current events, they're not just coincidences."

Father Samuel stood, his frailty apparent. "Be cautious, my children. The path you tread is fraught with shadows from the past. I will pray for your guidance."

As Dr. Greensberg and Dr. Phillips left the office, the weight of history and the potential gravity of their discovery loomed over them. They stepped out into the daylight, their resolve strengthened, ready to uncover the secrets that lay hidden in the past.

On the other hand, an ordinary day was about to take a series of extraordinary turns.

Tom, an experienced electrician, was high up on a telephone pole, his mind partly on the job and partly on the dinner plans he had later that day. Below, his colleague Mike shouted a warning, but it was too late. Tom's foot slipped, and in a moment, he was falling. The electrical shock from the transformer he struck on his way down was fierce and unforgiving.

Mike was on his phone in an instant, voice shaking. "We need an ambulance at 5th Street! Electrical accident, he's fallen… he's not moving!"

Across town, Alex revved his motorcycle, relishing the freedom of the open road. As he navigated a busy intersection, a car sped through a yellow light, striking him with brutal force. He was hurled through the air, crashing through the windshield of an SUV. The driver, a woman named Sandra, screamed in shock, her hands trembling on the steering wheel.

Around them, bystanders gathered, one calling out urgently, "Someone call 911! He's badly hurt!"

High above the city, a small plane piloted by Sarah, an experienced aviator, was navigating a challenging flight path. Suddenly, a gust of wind caught the plane off guard, the rudder jamming and sending the aircraft into a dangerous descent. Sarah battled with the controls, her co-pilot shouting, "Mayday, mayday! We're going down!"

The plane crashed into a dense thicket of trees. Sarah, injured and dazed, could feel the sharp pain of a tree branch impaled in her chest.

In the ICU of the city hospital, Dr. Menita stood over Tom, who had been rushed in earlier. His condition was critical, but as he received the blood transfusion, something miraculous occurred. The burns on his arm and chest began to heal at an astonishing rate, the wounds closing before the medical team's astonished eyes.

"Dr. Menita," a nurse called out, her voice a mixture of disbelief and awe. "Look at his wounds… they're healing!"

Dr. Menita, her eyes wide, could barely believe the sight. "This… this is remarkable. We need to document every detail of his recovery."

Meanwhile, Alex, now in another part of the hospital, was also experiencing a miraculous recovery. His injuries, which had been life-threatening moments ago, were now healing rapidly after the transfusion.

A young resident, Dr. Harper, turned to a colleague, amazement coloring her voice. "Have you ever seen anything like this? His wounds... they're healing as if by magic!"

Sarah, too, found herself in a similar inexplicable situation. As the blood transfusion flowed into her veins, the branch that had impaled her seemed to cause less and less damage. The bleeding stopped, and her wounds began to mend in a way that defied medical logic.

While observing her recovery, Dr. Phillips spoke into his recorder, his voice steady but filled with wonder. "Patient's recovery is unlike anything in the medical literature. The rate of healing is extraordinary."

Dr. Menita convened an emergency meeting with her team. "I've just witnessed something I can't explain scientifically," she said, her voice charged with a mix of excitement and seriousness. "We need to investigate these cases thoroughly. There's a pattern here that we can't ignore."

The medical staff exchanged looks of bewilderment and curiosity. Unbeknownst to its residents, the city was on the cusp of uncovering a medical mystery that could change the very foundations of science and medicine.

***

The night was cool and quiet outside the city's main medical research laboratory where Detective Jeffrey Thompson was. His features were shrouded in the darkness as he inspected the security measures with a calculated gaze.

He made his move, skillfully bypassing security systems, his mind fixated on one goal – obtaining the identity of the miraculous blood donor. Inside the lab was a labyrinth of high-tech equipment and sterile corridors. Thompson moved with the stealth of a seasoned detective, his senses alert.

Safely outside, Zachary's first instinct was to call Courtney. He dialed her number, his hands trembling. The call went to voicemail, and he left a frantic message. "Courtney, it's urgent! You're in danger! They know about you. Call me back as soon as you get this!"

Without wasting another moment, Zachary darted to his car parked in the shadows. He started the engine and sped off, glancing constantly in the rearview mirror, fearing that Thompson might be on his tail.

His destination was clear – the police station. He needed to report what he had witnessed and to get protection for Courtney. As he drove, his mind was a whirlwind of fear and concern for Courtney's safety and the implications of her unique blood.

Upon reaching the police station, Zachary burst through the doors, his words tumbling out in a torrent of urgency. "I need to report a break-in… a shooting… and my girlfriend, she… she might be in danger!"

The officer on duty, taken aback by Zachary's disheveled appearance and frantic demeanor, tried to calm him. "Slow down, son. Tell me everything from the beginning."

Zachary recounted the night's harrowing events, his voice a mixture of fear and desperation. The officer listened intently, jotting down notes. "We'll send a unit to the lab immediately. But about your girlfriend, do you think she's directly in danger right now?"

"I… I don't know," Zachary stammered. "But she's connected to all this. She's the blood donor, the one with the healing properties."

The revelation hit the officer like a shockwave. "Wait here," he instructed, moving quickly to relay the information.

As Zachary waited, his anxiety mounting, the front door of the station opened. In walked Detective Thompson, his face a mask of calm that did little to hide the sinister glint in his eyes. Zachary's heart sank. The predator was here, in the heart of safety.

Panicking, Zachary slipped out a side door, his mind screaming for him to get to Courtney before Thompson could piece together the puzzle. He jumped into his car and peeled out of the parking lot, his only thought to reach Courtney and keep her safe from the impending storm.

The city lights blurred past him as he drove, each passing moment an eternity, each thought a prayer for Courtney's safety. Little did he know, the wheels of destiny were already turning, drawing them deeper into a mystery larger than either of them could have ever imagined.

Unaware of her blood's extraordinary value, Courtney entered the blood donation unit with her friends Tamara and Candace. The room was filled with the soft hum of machines and the quiet chatter of donors and nurses.

"Hey, Courtney, you're up next," one of the nurses called out, smiling warmly.

Courtney took a seat, rolling up her sleeve. "I'm just glad to help out. Never know who might need this," she said, a hint of pride in her voice.

As the needle pierced her skin, she chatted amiably with the nurse. "Does it always stay this busy?"

The nurse nodded, securing the tube. "Yes, especially now. There's been a spike in demand for blood donations. You're doing a great thing."

Unbeknownst to Courtney, her donation today was more significant than she could ever imagine. As her blood flowed into the bag, she was, in fact, giving the gift of miraculous healing.

Meanwhile, outside, Detective Thompson sat in his car, his eyes fixed on the entrance of the blood donation unit. He had been following Tamara, mistakenly believing her to be the miraculous donor. His phone buzzed – a message from Domenico, urging him to confirm the identity of the donor.

Thompson stepped out of his car, his gaze narrowing as he saw Tamara exiting the building. He followed at a distance, blending into the crowd.

As Thompson tailed her, his phone rang. It was Domenico, his voice laced with urgency. "Do you have her? Is it the girl?"

Thompson kept his eyes on Tamara, speaking quietly. "I'm following her now. I'll have confirmation soon."

Inside, Courtney finished her donation, feeling a sense of accomplishment. She stood up, slightly dizzy, and the nurse offered her a reassuring smile. "Take it easy. Have some juice and rest for a bit."

As Courtney sipped her juice, she chatted with Candace and Tamara, completely oblivious to the fact that her simple act of donation was about to set off a chain of events that would change her life forever.

Outside, Thompson's pursuit of Tamara led him further away from the true miracle donor. He watched as Tamara met up with friends, none the wiser to the precious gift that Courtney, who had just left the unit, unknowingly possessed.

Still on the phone with Domenico, Thompson muttered, "I'm on her trail. This has to be the one."

CHAPTER 9

Veiled Dangers

Courtney, her heart racing with fear, clutched her phone tightly as Zachary's words echoed in her mind. Amid the bustling crowd of Midtown Mall, she felt a chill of isolation, knowing that danger lurked unseen.

"Zachary, I… I'm at the mall," Courtney stammered into the phone, her voice barely above a whisper. "You're saying my blood… it's healing people? And someone's after me because of it?"

On the other end, Zachary's voice was a mix of urgency and fear. "Courtney, listen to me. I'm not joking. The blood samples, the miracles, it all leads to you. Someone murdered Mr. Gregory at the lab, and I… I think they're after you next."

Courtney's eyes darted around, scanning the faces in the crowd. "I don't understand. This can't be happening. I'm just a college student, Zach. How could my blood be… special?"

"Trust me, Courtney. I saw the lab results myself. Your blood is unlike anything we've ever seen. You need to be careful. I'm coming to get you," Zachary replied, his voice tinged with determination.

Hanging up, Courtney's fingers fumbled as she dialed her parents, the weight of Zachary's revelation bearing down on her.

"Mom, something's happened," Courtney began, her voice quivering. "Zachary says I'm in danger because of my blood. He says it's… special, that it's been healing people. And now someone might be trying to… to hurt me because of it."

On the other end, Mother Malveaux's voice was a mixture of confusion and concern. "Courtney, honey, slow down. What are you talking about? Special blood? Are you hurt?"

"No, Mom, I'm not hurt. But Zachary's boss was killed, and he says a police officer might be involved. He's coming to get me. I'm scared, Mom," Courtney replied, her voice breaking.

Mother Malveaux's tone shifted, steel lacing her words. "Listen to me, Courtney. Lock yourself in a bathroom or a store. Don't go anywhere until Zachary gets there. Your father and I… we'll figure this out."

The line clicked as Courtney's mother hung up, leaving her alone amidst the sea of oblivious shoppers, her mind racing with fear and confusion.

Meanwhile, Mother Malveaux moved with a newfound urgency, her maternal instincts in overdrive. She hurried to the closet, her hands steadying as she retrieved the handgun they kept for home protection. The weight of the firearm in her hand was both a comfort and a grim reminder of the reality they now faced.

As Courtney waited, hidden in a corner of the mall, each passing second stretched into an eternity. The crowd's murmur was a distant echo compared to the pounding of her heart. She clutched her phone, praying for Zachary to arrive before the unseen danger found her first.

***

Under the clear sky of the city, Dr. Kathy Greensberg stood with her phone pressed to her ear, a look of deep concern shadowing her features. Dr. Carla Menita's voice, filled with urgency and disbelief, echoed from the speaker.

"Kathy, you won't believe this. We've identified the blood donor with the miraculous healing ability. She's a 19-year-old girl named Courtney Malveaux, living right here in the city," Dr. Menita's voice crackled through the phone.

Dr. Greensberg's eyes widened in shock. "That's incredible, Carla. And alarming, given the recent events."

Dr. Menita continued, her voice laced with anxiety. "There's more. The lab supervisor was killed last night. And now, the lab technologist, Zachary, is missing. It seems like someone's desperately trying to cover their tracks."

Dr. Greensberg's mind raced with the implications. "This is bigger than we thought. I've just spoken to the Priest at the Catholic Diocese. History is repeating itself, Carla. This has happened before, and now Courtney and her family are in grave danger."

Dr. Menita, on the other end, paused, digesting the news. "Do we have an address for Courtney?"

"We're working on it as we speak," replied Dr. Menita. "A police unit will be dispatched to her home for protection. But there's something else bothering me. How did this information leak? We've been so careful."

Standing nearby, Dr. Phillips said, "It has to be someone on the inside. The only others who knew about the blood donor were us and Bryan Domenico. And if he's involved…"

Dr. Menita's voice was tense. "We can't rule out anything at this point. The stakes are too high. I'm afraid our phone lines might be compromised."

"Then we must communicate discreetly, Carla," Dr. Greensberg suggested. "Use a secure line or a different phone. I'm heading to meet Bishop Abaracus. He's our best shot at finding Courtney and her family safely."

"I'll do that, Kathy. Keep me updated. We're in a dangerous situation and need to tread carefully."

The call ended with a solemn promise of vigilance. Dr. Greensberg looked out over the city, the weight of their responsibility heavy on her shoulders. The race against time to save Courtney Malveaux had just intensified.

***

Dr. Kathy Greensberg and Dr. Jon Michael Phillips stood in the serene meeting room of the Priesthood location, awaiting their audience with Bishop Abaracus. The room exuded a sense of ancient wisdom, its walls adorned with symbols of a bygone era. The Bishop, a tall, dark-skinned man with a presence that commanded respect, stood on the balcony, absorbing the last rays of the setting sun.

As the Bishop turned to greet them, Dr. Phillips stepped forward, urgency in his voice. "Bishop Abaracus, I'm Dr. Jon Michael Phillips, and this is Dr. Kathy Greensberg. We urgently need your help locating the family of Simon's seed. We fear for their safety, especially a young girl named Courtney Malveaux."

Bishop Abaracus nodded, his expression solemn. "I'm aware of the situation. The sacred family has been under our watch since the beginning of the miracles. Unfortunately, we lost contact with them after the death of our presiding Bishop. Since then, their records and whereabouts have been concealed for their protection."

Dr. Greensberg questioned the necessity of such secrecy. "But why hide a trait that could revolutionize human health?"

Bishop Abaracus spoke first, his voice carrying a gravitas that filled the room. "Don't you see the evil of mankind?" he began. "Man has killed what he wants to destroy for power and money from the beginning of time. If someone gets the sacred family blood, imagine the lengths any government or evil company would go to harness its power. The torment and torture the sacred family would endure would be unimaginable. This is why the great Disciples of Jesus Christ were hunted and killed as well."

Dr. Phillips, absorbing the heavy truth in the Bishop's words, inquired, "Bishop Abaracus, is the sacred family the last line of Simon of Cyrene? And if so, how have they managed to exist all this time with this miracle blood and conceal its power?"

Bishop Abaracus nodded solemnly. "Yes, the sacred family is indeed the last of the offspring of the seed of Simon of Cyrene, also known as the seed of Simeon. Simon of Cyrene is the African man who carried the cross and helped our savior, Jesus Christ, bear the sins of the world to Calvary. When Jesus prayed for the strength and courage of Simon, the living blood of Jesus baptized him, converting him as a disciple through this sacred experience. Simon of Cyrene is unique; he is the only man to have helped Jesus with the cross and the only one to have the living blood of Jesus cover his hands and body while Jesus was alive. This sanctified Simon, transforming his life. From that time till now, the seed of Simon of Cyrene has been blessed by the healing blood of Jesus for all time."

Intrigued, Dr. Greensberg questioned, "What role does the Zebulon Priesthood play in protecting the seed of Simon?"

"The Priesthood of Zebulon," the Bishop explained, "was established specifically to protect the sacred healing powers of the seed of Simon of Cyrene. Our High Priest Zebulon, who knew Simon in Rome, offered to protect his family after the death of most of the Disciples of Jesus Christ and the beheading of the Apostle Paul. He knew the vulnerability of Simon's lineage and ordained the Ethiopian Priesthood to swear an oath to protect and care for the sacred family. All Zebulon Bishops and Priests have upheld this oath for over 2,000 years in honor of High Priest Zebulon of Ethiopia."

Dr. Phillips, seeking clarity, asked, "Is the power of the sacred blood truly real, Bishop Abaracus? And why was it not acknowledged by the Pope and others?"

Bishop Abaracus sighed deeply, a hint of sorrow in his eyes. "You must understand, Dr. Phillips, this was the very start of the church. Many were seeking power and influence. Simon of Cyrene's story had to be mentioned because of the many witnesses to him carrying the Savior's cross. However, the churches and congregations in Rome that Simon and his family established were not recognized, as the doctrine of the church was being formed for power and influence. The Roman government terrorized and killed many saints for power and domination. High Priest Zebulon observed this and knew Simon was vulnerable. So, he protected him with his military of dedicated men and created an order of sacred Priests to protect Simon of Cyrene and his family. High Priest Zebulon admired Simon's dedication to establishing churches as commanded by Jesus Christ and kept the wisdom and observation of the Original Hebrews from Moses' day in the Old Testament."

Dr. Greensberg pondered, "How do we protect them from those seeking to exploit this gift?"

"We have a network of men discreetly guarding the girl. They've been tracking her movements without direct interaction," the Bishop revealed.

Dr. Phillips asked, "How do we distinguish your men from those with ill intentions?"

Bishop Abaracus pointed to his own attire. "Our priests wear brown suits adorned with an olive leaf, similar to mine."

Dr. Greensberg sought confirmation of Courtney's current location. "Is she safe right now?"

After a brief call, Bishop Abaracus assured, "She's in the market district, in public, and safe for the moment."

"Let's hurry," Dr. Phillips urged, "We need to ensure her protection."

As they prepared to leave, Bishop Abaracus imparted a sacred symbol and a whistle for emergencies, assuring them of the Priesthood's support.

"We will protect her with our lives," Dr. Greensberg promised, a sense of honor and responsibility in her voice.

**

Detective Jeffrey Thompson, his face etched with tension and frustration, sat hunched in a secluded corner of the police station. He dialed Bryan Domenico, his voice heavy with the weight of his actions. The lab incident had spiraled out of control, and Thompson knew he was in deep trouble.

"Bryan, we've got a major problem," Thompson began, his voice strained.

Bryan Domenico's response crackled through the phone, "What problem? Speak up."

Thompson hesitated, then confessed, "I went to get the blood samples at the lab. There was someone there… I had to shoot him."

Domenico's shock was evident even through the phone. "You shot him? You were just supposed to get the samples and the girl's identity. What have you done, Thompson?"

Thompson's frustration boiled over. "The guy was in the way. It was a split-second decision, Bryan. We've got a bigger mess now."

Domenico's tone turned cold and commanding. "You better fix this, Thompson. Where's the girl? Did you get any leads?"

Thompson paused, then admitted another mistake. "No. There was a witness, Zachary, from the lab. He saw everything and escaped."

Domenico's anger was clear. "Find Zachary and the girl, Thompson. And clean up your mess."

Thompson replied with a sinister undertone, "I've taken care of one girl. She's in your warehouse. But there's more. Zachary's our key to finding Courtney, the girl with the miracle blood."

Domenico was incredulous. "My warehouse? What have you done, Thompson?"

The detective's voice turned cold. "I had no choice. The girl resisted; things got out of hand. But we can still salvage this. I'll track down Zachary and Courtney. You deal with the warehouse situation."

Domenico's frustration was evident. "This is beyond what I signed up for. I'm a government official, not a criminal mastermind."

Thompson's response was chilling. "It's too late for second thoughts, Bryan. We're in this together. Clean up the warehouse. I'll handle the rest."

As the call ended, the gravity of their situation hung heavily in the air. Detective Thompson stood up, his mind set on a dangerous path, while Bryan Domenico faced the daunting task of erasing the evidence of their crimes.

***

Dr. Carla Menita, accompanied by a uniformed police officer, approached the Malveaux residence. Her heart raced, not only from the urgency of the situation but also from the unknown reaction she might face. The usually serene neighborhood now felt like a stage for an unfolding drama.

Mrs. Malveaux, her voice trembling with a mix of fear and resolve, confronted Dr. Menita and the accompanying police officer by Priest Jeremiah, released his grasp. Courtney stumbled back, her heart pounding in her chest, unharmed but visibly shaken. The assailant fell to the ground, writhing in pain, his arm grotesquely twisted and broken, a stark testament to the Priest's formidable power and the seriousness of their mission to protect Courtney at all costs.

Meanwhile, Zachary and Detective Thompson were embroiled in a fierce struggle. Thompson's face twisted in rage, his movements erratic and dangerous. Zachary, driven by a potent mix of fear and an instinct to protect Courtney, matched Thompson's aggression with determined resistance.

"Are you alright?" Priest Jeremiah called out, his eyes darting between Courtney and the violent tussle.

"Yes, I'm not hurt! Please help Zachary! That man is trying to kill us!!" Courtney's voice shook with terror as she watched the scene unfold.

Priest Jeremiah moved swiftly, his gaze locked on the escalating conflict. Sensing his plan falling apart, Detective Thompson desperately reached for his gun. But his actions were anticipated by the trained eyes of Priest Marcellus. With a swift motion, he hurled a star-shaped blade with deadly accuracy, striking Thompson in the neck. Blood erupted from the wound as Thompson discharged a stray bullet into the air before collapsing, the life draining from his body.

The distant sound of police sirens grew louder, signaling the approaching end of this harrowing ordeal. Courtney and Zachary, still shaken, turned to the priests with gratitude in their eyes.

"Thank you for saving us. But who are you guys?" Courtney asked, her brows furrowed in confusion and curiosity.

Priest Jeremiah stepped forward, bowing his head respectfully. "We are guardians of your bloodline, Miss Courtney," he revealed solemnly.

"What?" Courtney replied, her voice laced with disbelief and intrigue.

"Let us move somewhere safe, and I will answer all of your questions," Jeremiah urged, his tone gentle yet firm.

Zachary and Courtney exchanged a glance, a silent agreement passing between them. They nodded in unison, accepting the Priest's proposal.

As Dr. Phillips and Dr. Greensberg arrived at the chaotic scene, their eyes quickly took in the grim aftermath – Detective Thompson's lifeless body, the injured adversaries, and the enigmatic priests preparing to leave. Recognizing Courtney among the turmoil, they rushed to her side.

"Are you alright, Courtney?" Dr. Greensberg asked, her voice laced with concern.

"We're okay, thanks to them," Courtney gestured towards the priests.

With a shared sense of urgency, Zachary and Courtney led the way to Zachary's car, their minds burdened with worry and unanswered questions. Dr. Greensberg and Dr. Phillips followed closely, their thoughts racing, pondering the revelations of the day and the uncertain future that lay ahead.

CHAPTER 10

The Legacy of The Living Saint

The air was thick with tension in Zachary's car as Courtney's phone vibrated urgently, breaking the silence. Her eyes widened in shock as she read the message displayed on the screen. It was from Tamara, her friend, who was in dire straits.

"Courtney, help me. I've been kidnapped. I'm in Bryan Domenico's building, in the medical lab basement. Please, hurry," the message read.

Zachary, who had been focused on the road, glanced at Courtney, noticing the sudden change in her demeanor. "What's wrong, Courtney?" he asked, concern lacing his voice.

"It's Tamara," Courtney replied, her voice trembling with urgency. "She's been kidnapped and is somewhere in Bryan Domenico's building."

Zachary's face tensed with worry. "Courtney, we need to be cautious. It's too dangerous for you to go there. We should head to the safe building Dr. Menita set up for us."

But Courtney was resolute, her eyes fixed on her phone as she tapped rapidly, activating her friend finder app. "I can't just leave Tamara there, Zachary. She's in danger because of me. I can see her location here on my phone. She's only ten minutes away."

Zachary knew arguing with Courtney was futile when she was this determined. He sighed, resigned. "Okay, we'll go get her. But we need to be careful."

***

In a different part of the city, Bryan Domenico, flanked by three armed men, hurried into his building, a look of urgency etched on his face. He was unaware of the tumultuous events that had unfolded—Detective Thompson's death and Tamara's desperate call for help. His only focus was on erasing any evidence that could tie him to the kidnapping or the murder of the girl.

Meanwhile, Dr. Greensberg was on a call with Dr. Menita. "Carla, we've found Courtney," she reported. "We're following her to a building now. It looks like she's headed somewhere to help a friend in trouble."

Dr. Menita, shocked by the update, responded, "What! I told Zachary to take them to the secure health core building. There must be something making them deviate from the plan."

Dr. Greensberg continued, "Detective Thompson is dead. It seems he was trying to use Courtney's blood for his own gain. Zachary mentioned he also killed his boss at the lab."

Dr. Menita processed this information. "It was Detective Thompson on the video surveillance. Oh my God… was he working with Bryan Domenico?"

Dr. Phillips added, "It looks like it. We are approaching Bryan Domenico's building now. Bryan's car is parked here."

Dr. Menita urged caution, "Please, don't do anything rash. I am calling the police and heading there now. Just stay safe and wait for the authorities before entering the building."

As they parked near Bryan Domenico's building, Dr. Greensberg and Dr. Phillips prepared themselves for what might lie ahead. The government health clinical facility building stood ominously in front of them, hiding the dark secrets within its walls.

The gravity of the situation weighed heavily on them. The pieces of the puzzle were falling into place, revealing a sinister plot that went deeper than they had imagined. The lives of innocent people hung in the balance, and they knew that every second counted. With a mix of determination and trepidation, they readied themselves to face whatever awaited them inside. The shadows of the building seemed to loom larger as they took their first steps toward uncovering the truth.

Courtney and Zachary pulled up to Bryan Domenico's building, parking along the street. Bryan Domenico's car was noticeable in the parking space; a van was ominously parked nearby. Soon after, Dr. Greensberg and Dr. Phillips arrived, pulling up alongside Courtney and Zachary.

"Courtney... what are you doing here?" Dr. Greensberg asked, concern etching her features. "You were supposed to go to the secure location Dr. Menita set up for you."

Courtney's voice, firm yet tinged with fear, responded, "Listen to me, please! My friend Tamara is in that building. She's been kidnapped. She texted me from there, and I have to try to save her. I can't not help her!"

Dr. Phillips, worried, interjected, "Courtney, we need to think about your safety. We can keep you safe and wait for the police."

Undeterred, Courtney stood her ground, "I feel that Tamara is in there, and I need to do something to save her. I don't know where my help came from at the mall, but I only hope they are with me now. Above all, the Lord God is with me, and I will save Tamara from these evil men."

Zachary, resolute and focused, added, "Courtney, I'm with you. Let me get my crowbar from my trunk. I'll always protect you. Has Tamara tried to text you again?"

"Thank you, Zachary," Courtney said, her voice grateful yet anxious. "No, but I will call and text her while we go in. We may be able to hear the phone ring. She said she was in the lower level, like a lab area."

Dr. Phillips, determined, said, "I'll go with you. It seems you have God and some great priests to rescue you. As a sacred person of God, I feel safer around you than out here alone. We're with you."

Dr. Greensberg nodded, "Yes, Courtney, I'm with you too. We'll help save your friend. Bishop Abaracus gave me a whistle to blow if we need the Priests of Zebulon, who guard and protect you. I believe we'll have their protection if needed."

Courtney's voice, a mix of determination and newfound purpose, concluded, "I feel my life has just begun today. Those priests are amazing, and I'm so thankful to them for protecting me. We will be alright. I know God will allow me to do some good with my abilities. I trust in God for that protection."

With this, the group prepared to enter the building, facing the unknown dangers that lay ahead, united in their determination to rescue Tamara and confront the evils within.

***

Courtney, Zachary, Dr. Greensberg, and Dr. Phillips approached the government health clinical building. Upon reaching the door, they realized it was locked. Zachary wielded a crowbar without hesitation, prying open the door to grant them access. The building, though lit, echoed with a hollow, eerie silence. The group moved swiftly through the halls, checking each room on the first floor, finding them empty and silent.

Proceeding with caution, they descended the stairs, their footsteps barely audible. The second floor was just as deserted as the first. They continued to the third floor, where they were greeted by a chilling sight—hospital beds in empty rooms, adding to the unsettling atmosphere.

As they descended further to the fourth floor, their tension heightened. Suddenly, they noticed two men entering a lab room. The group quickly hid behind some shelves, their hearts racing. Unbeknownst to them, the Priesthood of Zebulon was following, never too far behind, especially from Courtney.

In the lab room, a horrifying scene unfolded. Bryan Domenico, frantic and unaware of Detective Thompson's demise, attempted to make a call that went unanswered. He then heard a movement from a tarp-covered figure. Underneath, a young girl, bruised and injured from a fall and a brutal assault, struggled to free herself. She screamed in terror upon seeing Tamara tied up and gagged.

Hearing the girl's scream, the group knew they had to act. Zachary's voice, filled with determination and urgency, instructed, "We have to move now! Someone is screaming. I'll lead with the crowbar. Courtney, you get Tamara and head to the stairs or elevators. Dr. Phillips, you watch my back against any of the guys that might harm Courtney. Dr. Greensberg, please help Courtney."

Courtney, her voice trembling yet filled with prayerful hope, said, "I feel we will all be alright… God, please don't let us die today… Please, God, send us help."

Dr. Greensberg, readying the whistle given by Bishop Abaracus, added, "I'm going to blow this whistle now. Hopefully, the Priests will intervene and help us, but we must act now to save your friend."

Resolving to protect the group, Dr. Phillips affirmed, "I've got your back, Zachary. Let's stick together and do as much as possible until help arrives to save Tamara and Courtney."

With a collective breath, they prepared to confront whatever lay beyond the lab room door, united in their resolve to save Tamara and face the unfolding nightmare.

***

Zachary, Dr. Phillips, Dr. Greensberg, and Courtney burst into the lab room where they had heard the scream. The room was a vortex of chaos and violence.

Zachary, leading the charge, swung the crowbar with force, striking one of the men in the head and sending him crashing to the ground. The impact echoed through the room. Dr. Phillips, following close behind, found himself face-to-face with another assailant. He took a hit to the face but managed to counterattack, landing a solid punch in the man's stomach and then striking his face. The man, reeling from the blows, kicked Dr. Phillips to the ground and reached for his gun.

In the meantime, Courtney and Dr. Greensberg, upon entering the lab, saw Bryan Domenico rushing into another room. Dr. Greensberg, remembering Bishop Abaracus's whistle, blew it. The sound it emitted was piercing, almost otherworldly, shattering the lab door's glass.

Suddenly, the Priests of Zebulon made their dramatic entrance, descending swiftly using latch hooks. They landed in the hallway and moved with purpose towards the lab room. One of the men, seeing the priests, panicked and fired his gun but missed. Priest Marcellus, with incredible speed and precision, threw a star-shaped blade, striking the gunman's hand, causing him to scream in agony and drop the gun.

In the chaos of the confrontation, the sounds of struggle and desperation echoed through the lab. Priest Jeremiah engaged in a fierce struggle, was suddenly stabbed in the side. His assailant, previously downed by Dr. Phillips, had regained his footing and seized the Priest in a chokehold. Jeremiah flipped the assailant over his shoulder with a swift and powerful move, freeing himself from the grasp.

At that moment, Adebijah, the third Priest, sprung into action. Drawing his blade with a swift motion, he thrust it into the chest of the attacker, ending his threat permanently. The assailant's lifeless body crumpled to the ground, marking a grim end to the confrontation.

Meanwhile, another man, injured but still dangerous, scrambled towards his fallen gun. As he aimed to fire, Priest Marcellus, with a keen sense of danger, deftly dodged out of the way. However, the bullet, careening off its intended path, struck Zachary in the back just as he was about to untie the kidnapped girls. Zachary's agonized cry filled the room as he collapsed, blood soaking through his shirt.

Reacting with lethal precision, Priest Marcellus launched his star-shaped blade, striking the gunman directly in the eye. The force of the blow sent the man reeling over a counter, where he lay motionless, his life extinguished by the deadly accuracy of the star blade.

Amidst the turmoil, Courtney rushed to Tamara, her movements fueled by urgency and concern. She worked feverishly to untie her friend, with Dr. Greensberg assisting her. Their focus was suddenly disrupted when Bryan Domenico burst into the room. In a desperate attempt to gain control, Domenico grabbed Dr. Greensberg, throwing her to the ground. The two struggled fiercely on the floor, with Dr. Greensberg's screams punctuating the tense air.

Dr. Phillips, seeing the danger, lunged at Domenico with ferocity. He landed a solid punch to Domenico's mouth, followed by a swift kick to his stomach and side. Dr. Greensberg managed to break free amidst the scuffle. But Domenico, relentless in his pursuit of control, pulled out his gun and fired at Dr. Phillips. The bullet hit Dr. Phillips squarely in the chest, sending him sprawling to the floor.

With a cold and calculating gaze, Domenico then turned his weapon towards Courtney and Tamara; the hostility in his eyes was unmistakable. The situation had escalated to a dire climax, with lives hanging in the balance.

"You think your blood will save you and your friends now, girl?"

Standing defiant in the face of danger, Courtney retorted with unyielding confidence, "I know you will not get out of this alive! And I am confident that you will not get away with this!"

In the heightened tension of the lab room, the unexpected arrival of Bishop Abaracus turned the tide. With a swift motion, he threw his spear with deadly precision, piercing Bryan Domenico's heart. At the same moment, Domenico's gun fired, striking Tamara, who collapsed to the ground just as Courtney freed her.

Domenico's body hit the floor, lifeless. The room fell into a sudden, eerie silence, broken only by Courtney's horrified screams. She looked around frantically, her eyes widening in fear as she saw Zachary, Tamara, a wounded priest, and Dr. Phillips, all injured and in pain.

Bishop Abaracus, with a calm yet commanding presence, approached Courtney. He consoled her, his voice resonating with a deep authority. "My child, you possess the greatest gift—the sacred blood of Simon of Cyrene. You are the seed of Simon, the last of his lineage blessed with incredible power. Your blood can heal them, just as it has healed others."

Visibly shaken and terrified, Courtney stammered, "Oh my God, Tamara's hit… Oh God, please let her live. What can I do? I don't know how to help them!"

Bishop Abaracus reassured her, "Believe in the power you hold. Your blood is sacred. When you first donated it, you did so with a heart full of prayers, and it healed many. Do the same now."

Dr. Greensberg interjected, "We can do a blood transfusion right here. This is a medical lab; we have what we need." She hurriedly moved to gather the necessary medical equipment—sterile needles, tubing, and donor blood tubes.

Courtney, her voice trembling with urgency, pleaded, "Please hurry! Zachary and Dr. Phillips are badly hurt. The priest, too… who are you people, and where did you come from?"

Bishop Abaracus responded calmly but firmly, "We are the sworn guards of the Priesthood of Zebulon, dedicated to protecting the sacred living saints of the Seed of Simeon. For over 2,000 years, since the day Jesus Christ our Lord died on the cross, we have been protecting your lineage. Your ancestor, Simon of Cyrene, was blessed with healing abilities, and you, Courtney, are his last living heir."

Dr. Greensberg, having found the necessary equipment, prepared for the blood transfusion, "Stay here, Courtney. I'll find the drawing needle and blood transfusion tubes. We can save them."

In the lab, Dr. Greensberg meticulously performed a blood transfusion on Courtney. As Bishop Abaracus and the unwounded priests watched in solemn prayer, Courtney's blood began its life-saving journey carrying its miraculous healing properties.

Zachary was the first to receive the transfusion. The transformation was miraculous. His wounds healed instantly, the bullet fell out from his body, and his pain vanished as if it had never been.

Next was Dr. Phillips. As Courtney's blood entered his system, his injuries healed in an almost visible cascade of recovery. The bullet expelled itself from his body, and he rose, completely healed.

Tamara, still lying on the floor, received her transfusion next. Her injuries mended before their eyes, restoring her to full health. The other girl in the room, the one who had been missing and was reported on the news, also received the transfusion. She, too, was healed, overwhelmed with gratitude for this unforeseen miracle.

Lastly, Priest Jeremiah received his transfusion. His stab wound, a grim reminder of the violent confrontation, healed instantly, leaving no trace of injury.

At that moment, Dr. Menita and Courtney's parents burst into the room, followed by the police. Relief and joy filled their faces as they saw everyone healed by Courtney's sacred blood.

The legacy of the sacred blood, now embodied in Courtney, promised a future filled with hope, healing, and a newfound understanding of her role in the landscape of humanity's spiritual journey.

The end.

ABOUT THE AUTHOR

Dr. John E. Bell is an accomplished Surgical Podiatrist Physician and Mental Health Counselor, Gulf War US Navy Veteran and published Author and life soul music artist. Dr. Bell also wrote, produced and directed the critically acclaimed award-winning independent film, "The Internal Mist of Love"(2013). He also wrote and directed the film, "I think I can be doctor, Rise of the Urbanites"(2017) based on his children's book, I think I can be a Doctor. Dr. Bell has a passion for various genres of literature and music and aspires to share his vision of creative interest that he feels driven to share in his life's experiences. Dr. Bell graduated Magna cum laude from his alma mater Morris College in Sumter, SC 1996. Dr. Bell also graduated from Strayer university with honors with a master's degree in health service administration in 2008. Dr. Bell completed his Podiatric Medical Doctorate degree at Kent State University School of Podiatry Medicine has been a practicing Surgical Podiatrist Physician for over 20 years graduating from Kent State University in 2003. Dr. Bell also enjoys his passion for Clinical Mental health Counseling and helping people find a better state of mind and wellness with confronting mental disorders, anxiety and stress with positive strategies to reduce the rate of suicide, stress and domestic violence. The life isolation and tragic crisis of the covid19 pandemic inspired Dr. Bell to achieve his Masters of Arts degree in Clinical Mental health Counseling from Liberty University in 2023. Dr. Bell currently practices both Surgical Podiatry and Clinical Mental Health Counseling in the West Tennessee metropolitan area including Memphis and surrounding county areas. Dr. Bell has written four previous books of literature including a children's book and even a book on urban relationship genre books and cultural awareness books as well. Dr. Bell's literature work continues to reach new heights in his latest great read, The seed of Simeon, Simon of Cyrene. Dr. Bell has made life-soul music that appeals to all walks of life. His music is about his experiences and cultural surroundings that have shaped his views of culture, life and relationships. All his music was recorded in the rich music town of Memphis at Royal Studios, Young Ave studios and with talented Memphis based music producers that helped to bring out his unique soul life music genre sound. His music work can be found on Pandora, spotify and Iheart radio. Dr. Bell's books of literature can be found on amazon books online. Dr. Bell has been on many TV interviews, Including Fox 13 news and many morning TV news shows, Radio and Pod cast appearances over the years. In his community Dr. Bell serves with many charity events, church auxiliaries and health fairs and scholarship fund raising events to raise money for aspiring young people that believe in education. Dr. Bell is a proud member of Phi-Beta-Sigma Fraternity Inc. Dr. Bell lives in the greater Metropolitan area of West Tennessee and has one daughter.